I Am A Destroyer

Yes, I Am A Destroyer

Mira Mattar

Litmus Press

UK edition published by Ma Bibliothèque, 2020

Hazem Harb, *Thorns No. 2* (2022), UV fine art unique prints layered upon acrylic inside plexiglass, 200 x 160 cm.

ISBN: 978-1-933959-74-0
LCCN: 2025016476
Cataloging-in-Publication data is available from the Library of Congress.

Design and typesetting by Carolina Ortiz

Litmus Press is a program of Ether Sea Projects, Inc., a 501(c)(3) non-profit literature and arts organization.

Litmus Press publications are made possible by the New York State Council on the Arts with support from Governor Kathy Hochul and the New York State Legislature. This project is also supported in part by public funds from the New York City Department of Cultural Affairs in partnership with the City Council. Additional support for Litmus Press comes from the Leslie Scalapino–O Books Fund, The Post-Apollo Press, individual members and donors. All contributions are fully tax-deductible.

LITMUS PRESS
925 Bergen Street #405
Brooklyn, New York 11238
litmuspress.org

ASTERISM BOOKS
568 1st Avenue South, Ste 120
Seattle, WA 98104
asterismbooks.com

The Soul's distinct connection
With immortality
Is best disclosed by Danger
Or quick Calamity —

As Lightning on a Landscape
Exhibits Sheets of Place —
Not yet suspected — but for Flash —
And Click — and Suddenness.

Emily Dickinson

for friends, dead and alive

It has been possible to fulfill the requirements by performing, with a minimum of effort, a series of repetitive tasks. Through this fulfillment I have both lost and gained approval, friendship, love, trust and employment in rhythms that varied in a pattern deemed natural. Held in an embrace of correctness, the head was laid on the pillow in the same way every night.

This was easier if I canceled my experience, if it could be called as much. Besides, I preferred it that way. Memory, if it could be called as much, was not what I needed most so I colluded in its erasure. I wanted to exist, so I was born every day. Living was for another life.

I got a nice personality: me. This ensured survival or something like it—good circulation. Now I could navigate more successfully the tepid, necessary spheres and join more evenly with the seductive delusions of others. It was their universals I loved most of all.

I tried to stop being a plague and became luxurious instead. Had I not succumbed to this, I would still be turning in a circle around the same febrile, unanswerable questions.

Aglow with the industrious and single-minded activity of self-preservation was I.

Beside me all along, keenly circling the ankles keening, was a suffering, whining thing. Quieting it was as easy as it was necessary. Gradually, it stopped talking, became a weighty, lumpen addition to my being and, through continued and committed neglect, eventually, like a gall, dropped off.

Finally I could walk without this stone in my shoe.

I have a name but it is not mine.

I believe in nothing and know less. I have few opinions and only very slight, petty, pedantic and even somewhat fabricated preferences—just to have something to say in company when I am among it. I start with the same sound every time.

To give an impression that there is something there, here, a heart, some character, I have found that it is enough to say an opinion and show solidity by adherence; to say no I prefer that one and point at it—to lay the fingers over the strange body shape and express some self. See, the gesture says with the sounds, I too have a history and self-knowledge, control, ambitions, anecdotes, a story and the will to tell it. There is even an attic of heirlooms cleansed and wrapped; no scattered journals, no diasporic dispersal.

I have physical attributes of particular colors and textures, and my childhood was as terrifying as yours, replete with things sprouting. I have an aversion to some foods and the place I grew up in has features.

What I have most of all, abysmal in the osseous matter and in abundance, is fear. It does not have to be summoned to be present, it undergirds. I am only intimate with my fears. It is a staunch and vital intimacy, refreshing as the cool side of the pillow.

My dearest fear is destiny—that everything is written, that the path is forged, word follows word, sentence follows sentence. I hear over and over that it is the nature of things to end—but all I see is bludgeoning continuity. Perhaps then what is called nature is only the word for vicious insistence, or, what continues ceaselessly is a thing more insidious than nature and more relentless than I. Any moments of upward motion, that heart-lifting sensation that articulates the heart, light breaking through clouds, etc., are only momentary glitches, shared hallucinations, dropped stitches . . . and though I suspect occasionally that to spy with suspicion those moments of seemingly upward or even sideways motion might also be foolish, with fear and suspicion as my idiot guides, how can I be sure of anything? Gravity is the only fact. To think otherwise would be embarrassing, childish—and *I* am an adult, all the forms tell me so. I am lucky I have my fear to guide me—and whether or not fear is or isn't a belief, is the concern of the psychologists and philosophers—and I am not interested in the theories of either.

This attitude, if it might be called as much, helps me slip flexibly through the narrow days—or perhaps it is the narrowness of the days which allows for this flexible slippage, duodenumous. In any case I have no reason not to stay almost daily for dinner at the home of my wealthy employer, having created an excuse or two to loiter until then, upon which I gorge myself at their lavish table, agreeing with their small and pointless comments, laughing at their cruel and lazy jokes, even sometimes joining them at the most banal and dangerous events called culture (or: the spoils of war)—for which I am duly paid.

My job is to help them maintain the vast soft cushion between themselves and anything hard so they would always land not only on their feet, but on the feet and hands of others, on their heads and on their hearts on and on thus creating beneath them a solidified mass. A household tutor is the part I play. I ease, that is my quality, greased. Now there is nothing to stop me torturing animals, neglecting and offending those who might be or become loved, and cruelly ensuring the body's devotion to the aesthetic and ideological strictures necessary for a modern life.

At best my behavior is irrelevant, at worst it is of an only mildly despicable strain. Either way, little alarm is caused.

In my room I have just enough space to arrange my possessions around my possessions, and maneuver myself around them, possessed. Belongings belong, navigated around and balanced. I slide alongside the machines.

Here, the bed is the desk, the desk is the kitchen table, the hob is the lighter, the kitchen counter is the desk, the chair is the table, the bed is the sofa, the windowsill is the bookshelf, the cupboard is the wardrobe, the seductive zone is behind the clogged ear, the tongue a mop, the floor groundless. Each is without qualities: the tap is not shiny, its water is not refreshing or watery; the bed is neither narrow nor wide; the bare bulb illuminates nothing.

One object only is one object only. It feels its hollow, spacious interior, it has a confident boundary—me, my skin is unreliable, wrongly thin and fat. Of things, I take care of this cup. I wash it carefully, I dry it gently, I put it in the best place, inverted. On occasion, I pluck flowers from some well-tended garden to feed it but in so doing the cup becomes a vase and its flowers become the flowers thrown onto the grave of the cup being slowly lowered into the earth. (I was weak again, in my longing.) The cup becomes the deadest, most mourned object here in my little graveyard of stricken words pointing, stupidly, towards nothing.

Daily I must remember to fold down the fold up table. It is a small piece of wood hanging by a hinge to the narrow countertop designated kitchenette and demarcated as such by the difference between dirty linoleum and stained carpet. The table is supported by a narrow leg attached vertically to the counter, which, once pulled out, gives something for the table to rest on and when tucked away allows the table to disappear neatly. I pull it out every day to eat at if I eat or to drink at if I am not drinking in bed. Usually I go to bed having forgotten to fold it away and when I wake almost always crash into it. Day after day it hits me in the center of the strange body shape leaving the same bruise on top of the same marbling bruise. It is always fresh, so I cannot even tell if time is passing.

For the room's only feature, the electric fireplace, broken, my mocking hearth, I know I am being charged £20 more than those in the rooms that lack this feature. On it I keep a few bottles of low-range off-brand alcohol lest someone should visit and, seeing the drinks on the fireplace, be reassured that I have other visitors to whom I serve these drinks—the stability of a cocktail hour, the glow of a roaring fire. I dust the plastic fern and put it out. When I notice the face in the mirrored surface coating a square of wall above the fireplace I think, both forlorn and proud, that even this fireplace has more character and history than I.

No cute animal or kitschy design adorns the small box beside the bed. It was not given to me by anyone I care or could care about, it does not come from an interesting or meaningful place, its materials have predictable provenances, its hinges function charmlessly, and no identifiable mood characterized the moments during and after its unintentional pocketing. It holds sleep's necessary paraphernalia: foam earplugs—the room is on a main road, the border between two ailing boroughs vainly braced for cleansing; a darkly colored eye mask—the street lamps cast the room in a nauseous orange glow come evening; and a pack of easily obtained prescription sleeping pills which, when combined with the right amount of alcohol, aid sleep. Soon a comfortable gag, a swimmer's nose peg, and the crushing weight of tonnes of water. It is important to relax.

Because I have grown weary of the faces peering in at me from the top deck of the bus, arranging, rearranging, I keep the fabrics mostly stretched. The stranger's greasy sleeping head thudding against the window or lolling affectionately along a shoulder; the future's glistening viscosity in hoardings around rubble; trees in wisps and blooms; friends peripheral and thinned by waiting till each day's end to buy hard bread rolls that bloat them cheaply. Above, below, to one side, to the other: hacking cough, thumping stick, woman barking, TV, fucking, a fist in a wall, hold music, teardrop, an animal kneading a breast, smashed dishes, slammed door, three morning kisses, a tooth pulled from the gums . . . and from the window softly reeking fox shit, gasoline, weed, meat.

When I peer from the back window into the yards of the shops below I see often a mischief of rats rummaging in the mingled waste of the kebab place, the Chinese takeaway, and the chip shop. If the creatures were stupid, weak, we would not have to turn our heads, we could enjoy the ennobling effects of our pity; our gaze could raise us, showing us the tenderness of our own hearts, the fatness of our empathy. We turn because we do not want to be faced with the congruity between intelligence and desperation. It disgusts. When I eat at these places, ordering in numbers, paying in coins, I spread the paper napkin grandly on my lap and feel a peculiar sort of delight.

After dark, I light a candle.

A blue eye hangs in a palm above my door.

I was not a demanding baby. My cries were communicative and not abstract. My tiny fists did not punch the air attempting to understand how to move through it. I suckled neatly, and my teeth, when they appeared and dropped out and reappeared in my head, were white, straight, and entirely blunt. As soon as was possible, and earlier than, according to the literature, is usual, I achieved full control of the functioning of my bladder, bowels, tear ducts, and other various, dripping glands. My organs performed their work. Even as a foetus I was a well-aligned ascetic.

They told me I was a girl and I believed them. It taught me who I may and may not love, how to arrive at femininity and what I may and may not invoice for.

Peered at and skirted I understood my love would always have a pleading tone, that a shirt would never fall predictably against my chest, and that the lineage of smiling was only a hook in the cheek.

It was a narrow road ahead of managing, maintaining and defending this stranger's body; of making it body beyond body—shitless and pissless, bloodless yet lustful, smooth, firm to the touch but unfeeling. Furniture, a pet, I populated dreams.

It was disheartening for mourning to be the first thing I learned. It began shortly after birth.

I heard I was from somebody else's memory of a place. Even for them it is slight—an idea, scaffolded by the memories of others, who are dying, fading into memory and losing their own. Jolts, a texture, sentiment, aroma, tar, mint, bullet. Though I was lucky to be born fatherless, both he and I wondered constantly who he was.

Around my neck was hung a key to a house that does not exist in a place that does not exist but still is teeming with people. It thudded against our chest exposing its lost hollow. Inside, embroidery ran between the fingers, jasmine exhaled at dawn, and even the knuckles had knuckles.

How then did the wall of books throb constantly its inimical names? To identify temporarily was how to deny denial, how to make our own. Particularity was temporal—but had it stagnated, congealed with its fists up, chapping in the wind or was this commitment?

Visible invisible on the deepest scrolls, turning inside the slickest geographies whose function is to make the *I am* of one into the *am I* of another, to manufacture cruel difference.

What appeared as nostalgia—watercolors of fields and peasants, fields and peasants in poems—was history held to the present. It wondered how to remember without sentiment, or with sentiment in the correct proportion. Both rubble and the words to name it are rubble.

Forgetting daily, I became skilled at survival. In secret, I nursed the difference between the broad splash of myth and the fine point of true story. If I was fighting, was it for a memory's memory or because of one?

Besides, what is the fight, the arousal, of the silent, scratching our hearts from a well-fed distance—complaining about limescale, about supermarket sushi?

What is the independence that is also catastrophe? The stars had been aligned usually, the skies were regular. This was a visitation, well-planned, choreographed. What is the birth certificate that is also obituary? Mourning was encouraged—but in private, at once, once, and for all. To seal, to forget. But how, when what keeps getting more lost keeps getting more lost?

Let go, don't dwell on it—but mama, where can we live? Baba, how can I love? Would home feel like relief, or the pressure to feel it; arrival, or the distress of unlifted distress? Would it be unnameable, unimaginably new? How can I belong to that which is not mine? Is return a paradox and belonging a getting owned? Still. Refusal is pathologized as psychotic, terrorizing, and commitment clings obsessive, a nag. Vulgar, as ordinary and necessary as housework. A fact. I would meditate on patience if it didn't take so long. My father also turned seventy in 2018. I knew to be held by time was to never be held in a tender embrace. I knew that to move was to move in the dark. I knew that having a home and homelessness were conditions of each other, not yet resolved in this world but oh! to have somewhere to rest our sensational bodies.

And "afterwards"—what will happen to all the built-up matter? How will residue be resolved? How will hate? Will it be stuffed into the sea and eventually break the surface with a shocking, toxic island? Will what is inside the sea fall and rot and perish and be swept into a cankerous pile? What choleric interludes will follow? Who will clean up? What false leap would empathy allow? What will we decorate with? What will become our symbols? What will we see when we look out of habit forever over our shoulder? Will we be enemyless now, and live in oblivious elevation? Will we mistake our pain for an incapacity to cause it? How could we let the air touch at last our little cavities, alveoli, and smile at it while still this same stuff weighs rancid over the world?

It was like a curse to learn that the most common dream was of a confident boundary, and that blood would describe the boundary's boundary. We want our own daddy to spank us, not for the neighbor to sneak in after school. Could not fatherlessness be imagined? And both imagining and dreaming be wrenched gently from hope? Victory tinged my tactless nightmares.

Melancholia began shortly after birth.

So that I could move smoothly like a worm I concluded that what I thought of or felt as domination was only the name for difference.

I got this cool new hat. I drafted a list of reasonable demands. I got to wear the clothes of the clothes of the people of my people and explain them on stage. Still, I did not understand why as I wept, others cheered.

I tried to loosen up but all it got me was admission, it felt like a pillow over the face.

I tried to be more fun, but fun kept feeling ruthless.

Routine is crucial. To be led instead by conflicting needs and desires, to have to listen to, identify, and choose between them as they multiply and fold in and out of possibilities and impossibilities; to have them at all or wonder why they are not being had, or to consider their sources; to act upon them or not, or not be able to, would be dangerous.

Do only what you must. Learn to ridicule desire, or if you cannot, learn to pathologize it. Perhaps only rubbing your head and little jaw—clamped around a plastic dummy drooling—against the calves of your lover come dinner time will do it, perhaps only literature will.

To walk, I wait for the green man, hard as a hero, and fall into step with whoever dares walk beside me. I walk in the same direction as the traffic so the opposite cars cannot humiliate me with their X-ray beams. To eat, I count chews and swallow after fifteen regardless of texture, risk of choking or pleasure. To fuck, I do as I must, timed to the predictable throb in the eyes of my lover. To feel, I laugh with others and cry when they do, I pat my belly and document it online, I groan on the first day of the week and smile on the last. I join in with the superstitions —mushroom, mushroom, mushroom. To love, I hate. To live, I pay my bills immediately and my rent a day early, and in my best handwriting promptly inform the council of any change in circumstances, relationship status, bowel habits. My rhythms are chronicled, my imbalances known.

I work hard to maintain this body and doubly hard to conceal its maintenance. I have studied images of bodies, internal and external. How can I ensure its harmony and functioning—that the vaginal tract goes safely up towards a necessarily fecund womb, that the appendix will not attack, that the lungs will bloom with oxygen (and what is in this oxygen? Microplastics and ammonia, carbon monoxide, sulphur . . .), that the bones will uphold me, that the enamels and keratins will protect, that the stomach will know what to extract and what to discard, that enough surface area for the acids to function optimally will be created, that even what I eat will not be rejected?

Under false names and addresses I have registered at numerous GPs, dentists, and opticians. The cells on my cervical wall will not begin a secret alliance with the doctor, the story of my teeth and gums will not eventually betray me, no ophthalmologist will puff air into my eyeballs twice, learning, over time, their specific flinching and measuring its normality. I make room for gloved fingers and greased speculums. I lay an extra place at the table and breathe when I'm told to. In detail and on schedule I describe my flossing technique to the dentists. They blush, impressed, remembering my tongue. My nose is stroked affectionately, I yelp cutely in the chair. Weighed down by lenses I lift my face to the green and red circles and try to steady their vortexing by clinging white-knuckled to the chair.

I even have my hairs cut and removed regularly. I believe with the stylists that we cook, eat, and vacate, that what is lost gets replenished. I create elaborate stories about a boyfriend who has steady employment and opinions about pubic hair. Before I cross any salon's threshold I practice the word "boyfriend" three times: boyfriend boyfriend boyfriend. I am loved and love, the future is possible and this is my body. I know who I want to win every reality TV show currently on air in the UK and USA and I can tell you why, I can tell you my opinion on the rest of the competitors and the names of their hometowns. I do what I need to do to get by, to pass.

I run ten miles three times a week and swim twice. It's the endorphins. Sickness is costly and care is no promise. My wellness will come from the inside out. My body is long, lean, plump, and girlish. I carry a rape alarm. We are silhouettes, asterisks—this is not what we meant by privacy. This is our horoscope. Our tongues are out and our fingers softening. Yes, my upkeep is expensive but the predictability of my debt stabilizes me. My favorite kind of balance is knowing that whatever goes out is always greater than whatever comes in.

I travel far across the city, cut it knowingly, concealing behind me the entrances to tunnels, altering the signage. I traverse the grimiest bowels, skirt the farthest wettest edges like a silverfish active only in the hallucinatory hours, to avoid becoming known, to avoid any collusion between my body and theirs, its.

Unknown, I am free as a gangrenous limb, amputated, so as not to infect the rest of the body. Senseless, without fingerprints even, a softly gulping ocean.

I am careful not to enjoy solitude—untethered from the constant narrations of others, quiet enough to have senses one at a time. I am careful not to enjoy medium or large sized gatherings, with the sensations mingling and becoming keen and soft and touching. I align with the dyadic focus. I search only for my twin.

It is important not to arouse suspicion, which will arouse fear, which will be diagnosed as criminal; but to also express some lifelikeness without which some alarming deficiency will be revealed: she showed no emotion on the stand, she does not play well with others—every appearance a trial.

I try to communicate in a regular manner. I use only ordinary words and gestures and do not pepper my speech with unfashionable eccentricities or my motions with excessive flourishes. I watch my limbs. Though it is not mine, I clean and cut the language diligently but still it is marked with blood. I employ its normal cruelty with dry eyes. I make and receive friendly tips, little advices—a straightened tooth, a pulled taut wrinkle. I am careful to represent online in text and image anything potentially significant before it happens, abandoning it half-felt, half-thought, myself half-feeling, half-thinking, my flesh to the wolves still beating.

Together we ensure the narrowing of emotion and of gesture, of appetite and of possibility; we adhere to forms so slim from which only blandness, catatonia, hunger and destiny can peek. Make room at the table, this is a feast of bones. I have been scraped and filled entirely with noise. Barely nervous.

Having observed over time others attempt to communicate, I started moving my hands as I had seen them move theirs. They did not do so on inconsequential words—prepositions, conjunctions—but on crucial ones—pronouns, possessives. "You"—an open palm gestures in your direction, a finger points out the perpetrator. (Everything is war here.) "We"—rarely used and if so only to bind and exclude; or with abandon, imprecisely, implicating and including with force, leaving the shy, the sick, the dead to roam the edges eternally. "They"—the gorgeous plural, the elusive, or the easiest erasure. "I"—the forced insatiable. In writing I punctuate normally and employ unsurprising paragraph breaks.

Gesture can betray and be dangerous. What a young boy is for example must resist snaking the hips to any alluring song. No flicking pillow cases. Truckish wrists. What a young girl is for example must learn to always look away first—tease, weeping. Cry efficiently to obscure your own vision. Look to the screens! Like each word, each gesture might lead to your death. I learned long ago about poise.

My hands are the hands of another, moved by the mind of another, under the will of another.

(Once:

if there is a soul it resides in the body's more oblivious motions, the appearance of movement without history. Or perhaps it is precisely soullessness, being bound to no essence, which allows these latent motions.

There are short tendons somewhere inside the calves that lift the heels a little too highly up with each step. There is the arrogant, supple ease of flipping a pancake, a cigarette in the corner of the mouth. There is the eye bending softly into love.

It is the noticing of these things—some lithe attention paid—it is the recognition of that attention and its unflinching return that ambles towards tenderness.

But surveillance strikes the body's liquid charge, hardening it along the lilac veins and blinding the clear eye of love.)

Irregularly, I refresh the insides and outsides. Cleaning returns me to I. There, waiting, bright and exterior. The interiors are matching and virile. Naked, I lick the edges, I swallow down the spiders and their webs. I too purloin, this box my home—like the orb weaver who ingests each silky morsel of its proteinous web after it has been devastated on something as crude as a nose. What is a home that is also a trap? Is it witty or efficient? Vengeful or necessary? My tongue tears and blisters. That I am drunk is only a feeble preference and secret. What? I am simply a woman cleaning her dwelling places at the weekend. A radio gurgle. Look at her, regular, waged. The pipes exhale. I set the scene for the possibility of another encounter:

My pail is divine. It is metal, steel and flares proudly up from its circular base. Its handle is pre-held, farmy, like it did the same thing every day and really. Filled with scalding water and vivid disinfectant I plunge into it a rough sponge and extract it, squeezing amorously. I drag it along my tongue once quickly and spit. I searched in many shops for dear sponge, I wanted it to match exactly the specifically vague old-fashionedness of the bucket. Eventually, in a vintage inspired homewares emporium it found me, oozing my name. For free it was mine, £8.99 off. Rough, beige, and bigger than my hand. Starting in a corner I scrub in the same rippling circular motions I use for gently applying face cream. I cover the space methodically on all fours until I am in the last corner, underneath a previously unseen web, studying another spider who broods, surveying me. I stand clit-fingered, employing the same reverberating circular motions I use for scrubbing and gently applying. From my unscrubbed corner I peek out through the fabrics—here it is impossible to tell if it is children or dogs being talked to—sit, come, good boy. Here it is impossible to tell if I move because I come or because the floor has dried.

Next, quickly robed, I tread to the shared bathroom with my products. I clean the sink and taps, leaving the taps on. I tie my hair up and kneel before the toilet to clean it, then wash my hands and kneel again, resting the index and middle fingers of my right hand far back in my throat. I close my eyes, relax my throat, and am quickly overcome. A bat leaps out. Banquets flash before my eyes, bones and cream, livers, figs. Capillaries burst and bloom along my cheekbones, the sweet patches no lovers kiss no more. My calorific intake flows through me, is blocked, returns, sickens, tires, induces naps, rises, is expelled. To know if my heart is still beating I want to see it pounding under the rack of my ribs. I corrode, teeth first. I come out of my mouth because words are too large, too small, too soft, too hard. This is not about targets, but it is targeted. I flush, wash my hands again, clean the toilet again, clean the sink again, wash my hands again, and brush my teeth. I have at this point often an urge to genuflect.

A colossal black dog presses his paws onto my chest.

This petty machine. Feed me, water me, empty me, love me, feed me, water me, empty me, love me, feed me, water me, empty me, love me. Grow and grow and still it mewls and squalls. The insides coming out everywhere, running nose and weeping eyes, bowels undoing and exploding, appendix panicking and poisoning, cells striking, rebelling and multiplying, wet lungs' phlegm hocked, veins bulging from the sphincter, nails fungal, sexual parts infected, the heart's uneven thud, extremities freezing, the constant dying and dropping away of hair and skin, the always rampant growth, the removal of grease and blood and dirt, the plugging and releasing, vessels narrowing and gasping, bones crunching against bones and aching, the nerves, the dust. Everything prone. It is an inherited pet not even providing the vague comfort of another creature padding softly around in the morning for its breakfast.

Newly emerged, the mouthless Luna moth will live for one week only. Its eating all done in the earlier stages, now it must only ensure its reproduction.

There are always bruises on my chest from the dog.

With products chosen after a great deal of research and experimentation, staying up late on forums and writing off for samples—I do not want a murderous cleanliness but cannot afford it not to be—the hair and body are washed and the legs, arms, underarms, pussy, asshole, and eyebrows carefully shaved. I am washed into the drain, propelled wallwards, solidified, moved in flows and gushes—no stutters, no pratfalls—I am treated and re-used. With them in their homes I exist! Yearned for, present at morning and bedtime, for nervous spells and nausea, reached for in the night. Floral scents and deep hot spices, textures rough and luxurious, foams and blades, where is my smell? I cannot stand it, unmasked. Occasionally it catches me, shocking as the confluence of black seeds suddenly revealed at an apple's core.

As the depilatory cream works on my upper lip, chin, and sides of my face, I cut my nails into normal shapes. If I cut one shorter than another I have to even out the rest resulting frequently in bleeding fingertips which scab over quickly, are picked and eaten then bleed again. Only while it is damp can I reshape my hair into appropriateness. I floss and brush again and use the on-brand mouthwash for bloody gums. You wouldn't ignore bleeding from anywhere else, would you? Beautiful tears of beautiful blood unfurl along the beautiful woman's beautiful lily-white cheek. I do my smile. I am only a fugitive, an infant, learning language like the rest.

A drink is poured and drunk. The fabrics pulse in and out. The breeze has on it a scent of flowers, weed, petrol, cum, and meat. I close the window. An ant crawls over my toes, its heart a tube running through it. How did it survive the cleansing? It has two stomachs, one for itself and the other a crop, the social stomach which holds food to be shared with others. It is easy to squash. We had not noticed the pile our clothes was in was on top of an ant hill . . . dressing again in the sunlight we realized our trousers were teeming with ants. We brushed them off, laughing. I attempt to paint what's left of my nails in a neutral, barely visible color but a shade or so off chic—a too grandmotherly pearlescent, a pubescent pastel. How old am I?

I fail. As I remove the polish, the acetone diffuses into the room. I hold the open bottle in my hand and consider for a moment drinking it down, wondering what it may strip me of.

Exhaustion squirms right through even my threadiest veins.

My little extinctions are so revitalizing, my reproductions—so refreshing!

Perhaps a hand on the hip, a finger, index, to the pursed lips—may bring about thought, which may bring about action, decision. In the same way that what I wear might provoke a reaction (even if it is the reaction of no reaction) in those who may notice me and those who will be forced to look at me—sticking their fingers in to check I exist—I imagine that by assuming a thoughtful pose, thoughtfulness will be brought into being. I conjure I.

The empty pose will become known and so be filled, as a liquid fills all available space, or creates it through erosive action. Cuts a rill, gully, wrinkle. No space is left. Even echoes fill and drain. It comes into us even through our pupils and later when we piss it out of our faces we do not know what it is—this clamorous muck, humming and fried as out there. All the holes are tunnels being poured into. Everything meets in the bright, saturated bowels, the epiphanic, clogged center. The liquid petrifies us from the inside out. (Cannot hear, cannot see the way of that space.)

What would a me-like girl wear? Consult the professionals!

Clothes swing doomed, hanging.

I approximate their outfits. I try to pick ones that do not suggest we have dreams of motion beyond those promised by the clothes. It is a narrow skirt, I cannot run, the sleeves are tight, how am I to flail? However, it is important to appear as though I believe I can move. It is my aim to achieve the kind of comfort that enables only the slippage into whatever scenario without notice, ripple or friction. If I must lacquer and mold, crush and bind, I will lacquer and mold, I will crush and bind doubly, and doubly again.

For the face add make-up. I choose meticulously just the wrong shade of foundation, I draw the brows a tone too darkly, the blusher is a touch too vivid, the eyeliner an unfashionable color traced with a shaky hand across the stretched lids. Look, I too am sorry for my face. See, I try, I regenerate, I exfoliate.

Is this my bid for beauty? I walk like an apology mostly but sometimes I move forward in an affront, revolting.

Swallow: 75mg desogestrel, 10mg cetirizine hydrochloride, 60mg fluoxetine, 20mg hyoscine butylbromide, 300mg magnesium, 50mg vitamin B6, 5-10mg diazepam, 500mg naproxen, 100mg caffeine, 1000mg vitamin C, 4-5 drops propolis, 15 drops echinacea, 5000 iu vitamin D and 2 teaspoons psyllium husk dissolved in a half-cup of tepid water.

To meet the world takes style. To meet the world, I need style. To meet the world takes style equal to the world's style.

I am only a woman and it is only a supermarket airport shopping center filling station corner shop train station. I am only a woman and it is only a road without a curve splitting the earth in two sweet as a middle parting. There is nothing to fear.

They keep their places in towns. They keep the towns in their places, announcing them. Cube of town square, strip lit, criers expelled and ranting outside, small clothes misshapen by theft. Ubiquitous as flowers cropping up and smelling always the same, reliable, buttery. They protect themselves for us, suing for defamation. That the fattest pinkest wriggliest prawn requires fishmeal from slave owning suppliers to realize itself and then be realized, drizzled in lemon and garlic and arranged to have its brains sucked out is only a measure of the lengths gone to to ensure our nourishment. Isn't this romance? Pressed against the plastics vacuumed, water pumped and headless, ground and piled, laced with faeces, the discharge of abscesses, cobwebs, dead cockroaches, velvet flesh, rope of sinew erupting, hung and drained, gyrating skinlessly and bleached, frozen, flown, gutted, iced, each bloody peach a picker's tongue. I relish the phenylbutazone lingering in the meat, I want to ingest what has at least once been powerful. I relish even the traces of faecal bacteria in the desserts, I want to feel insides.

My heart beats to the rhythm of the coins thumping against my thigh as I walk checking labels as though I were checking labels. What is the relationship between our guts and the world, I wonder out loud to the checkout boy who quivers as I cup his pimpled face in my palm. I purchase the ingredients required to make a healthy meal.

I sit smiling at old women, myself, in their cafés afterwards. How old am I? The instructions are on the tea bag's label. I am grateful. The name of the person who picked the leaves is on the packet. I am reassured. The cup says its contents are hot. I am safe. I thrust my hands into the compartments of condiment sachets and line my pockets with mustard and ketchup and mayonnaise and sugar. I love sachets. I love condiments in sachets (I think they love me back). I suck at them on benches for dinner and dessert. I skirt the edges of the village where everyone is welcome.

After the time required to drink a cup of tea has passed, I leave, checking my dead watch telephone wrist pulse to suggest someone waits for me and this is our ritual. I live on and on. Outside, beyond the supermarket's view, I place the purchased items one by one into the bin. A homeless man watches me—agape.

God, I love loving a bargain!

I purchase a bedspread at seventy-five percent off and am high for hours after. Its design pertained to no particular particularity beyond that which is outside the predominantly available, and so was to be read as exotic. All it is is not what is. Only a violently and strategically imagined system of crude opposites stemming from an even more violently and strategically imagined system of crude oppositions makes it possible. I loved it.

Some people move with a light-footed delight. It is the glee of believing themselves the discoverers of something—something large—a continent, a species, algebra. It is these people who establish homewares boutiques where once were necessary pyramids of canned fruit, dried beans, every vegetable, types of sponge, smoking papers trilling in the breeze, thick curves of incense, fishes iced and fanned, each animal part, songs, bright curative candles, bread, clothing and luggage, persimmons, pomegranates, spells, spices, herbs, plungers, hairbands, every tea. It is one such person whose pedicured big toe, thrusting proudly out of colorful handmade leather sandals, is opportunistically pricked twice by the safety pin securing the strap of my bag to my bag as I crouch down to tie my tied lace. I wonder with her as I slip back up the silk or linen kaftan curving over her luxurious belly what was that what was that? A little mite, a little bite. As I pay I plead with the cashier to feel with me that we are almost equally different to the others, but we cannot feel together. At home I drop to my knees and cover her hands with small enthusiastic kisses, but nothing can really touch yet—there is only a book and its reader, the one in the hand of the other, clutched choking by its scruffless neck. The bedspread slides beautifully into the rope handled bag which I carry at my elbow in an attitude of pride. In my other hand, whose index finger wears a fake rose-gold ring I stole from the same place I bought the bedspread from, I hold an ethically sourced coffee from an independent retailer. Engraved on the ring are the words, *still this world*—imperative, lament; written on the coffee cup is a name—stranger, corpse. Coffee agitates my bowels but it completes this look. As a child, I trained myself to stop wincing. Authenticity is a boring problem.

Yesterday I relaxed my hair with an at-home chemical relaxer and though I burned off a patch in the middle of my scalp, enough hair of a still acceptable texture remained to cover up the raw flesh. With my legs crossed like a woman I sit on the train with the responsible coffee and the bag and the other like-women sitting with their legs and responsible coffees and bags. One admires my shoes, which are new, though belong to the person I work for, who has not yet noticed their disappearance—I cannot wait until she does. Nearby a man in his spacious body plays a mining game for small children on a device whose essential components are mined by small children. Like many other games the objective is imperial and the method seductive. People either side of him are flattened and out of shape, stuffed to the edges by his voluminously puffy gilet, a hunter. It is a practical item and so its color is a not too-rare one. It is of an orange that might be found in nature, say on the underwing of a common-ish butterfly. A gilet is natural to own. It is important that the orange is only common-ish—still rare enough to be expensive and speak what expensive items speak, muted. When I am him I will buy the biggest, most diamond-encrusted hoop earrings I can find, I will buy two hundred pound glass dildos and a designer fridge-freezer to put them in, no, no, I will buy a separate fridge-freezer just for sex toys, LSD, and champagne, I will buy lace underwear in both pale and garish colors which will peek out occasionally from beneath my clothes which will be intelligently layered and made of breathable, natural fabrics which will monitor my temperature ensuring constant cool, warm sweatlessness and whose back pockets will be studded with designer logos embellishing my impossible ass which will be so high and so pert on account of my personal trainer who I will see daily who I will sweat hard for and who will fuck me with my freezing cold well-lubricated two-hundred-pound glass dildo because I will not want his poor warm flesh inside my hot expensive cunt. I have done everything required to make the gilet's attraction to me likely and predictably its flat eyes light up with a thing so dull as I fantasize about lifting back my hair to reveal the chemical burn on my scalp and explaining in detail what will happen to me after I have finished drinking this coffee. Instead, the required behaviors are emitted.

Back in the box, this home, I consider for a moment sealing over my head and neck with duct tape the flexible plastic case enclosing the bedspread and waiting, but instead I lay the bedspread out. A camera pans over my hands as I perform this motion, no, a camera pans over the hands of a woman who does not have scabbed nubbins for fingertips as she performs this motion. I ignore the light plasticky smell clinging to the bedspread. I ignore the hours of labor some distant strangers have exerted in creating these thousands of embroidered flowers differing in size, atrocity, and degree of exoticism, or in overseeing or attending to the machines which embroider them. I ignore the undergrowth they make where friends may lay down. I ignore the dappled light that fell over us when we lay there. I lay. I dream: one thousand chapped and blistered fingertips hover over my new bedspread. One thousand hunched backs and narrowed eyes scour my new bedspread. One thousand drops of blood bloom into the one thousand vivid flowers of my new bedspread. One thousand vivid flowers grow out of my new bedspread and entangle me until I am pulled under, lost in their vines, until I disappear.

(As if this, as if this, as if this could.)

I arrive a little early but I am sure never to be the first or last. It is only a day off and there is nothing to fear. It is pay-what-you-can so I deposit a little fistful when no one is looking, distracted in the flow of arrivals. What I have paid in travel to pay-what-I-can here is an embarrassing equation. I greet the others with their mats and phones and faces and we perch in the changing room removing our winter coats, scarves, shoes, summer dresses, sandals, sunglasses; exchanging analogous observations about the weather, how tired we are and how the two may or not be connected. We are only women and it is only daylight. We greet our teacher meekly, shamed before her templic body, and nod again towards the window, signalling the weather, its effects—a keystone, or is it the microbiota in our guts? Or discipline? Or its lack? Is it writing? What is it to have devoted your life to a mistake? Deep breath. Belly breathe. Look, the secret is probiotic.

Oh community, strung up between the lampposts from our ankles for feast day. We lie for ten minutes just breathing. I try not to breathe too loudly or quietly. The ostentatious breathers are distracting, relaxing arrogantly, and I doubt the commitment of the reserved ones. We feel the breath enter and exit through the nostrils, imagining it passing over the tiny hairs in there, defining them one by one; we feel it fill our lungs from our abdomens up, each bronchial node illuminated, its selfhood aroused. We feel our chests rise, our hearts expand and be lifted on themselves towards the light. All the hearts are so full they smash into each other and bounce, retaining their shape—impermeable, zoned.

Had I wanted shattering, dispersal? To move without history, a ray, accidental and then gone. I wanted to be in the way of an ocean and ignored, turned, dragged along and carried—my littlest life wish. Let me be sand, let me be foam, bursting. But we are so okay. I am so okay. I am my own responsibility. I am full. I am light.

Shimmering afterwards still the bone-paved streets are studded white with broken glass and vomit constellated, disturbing civility ordinary violence shuffles mad, constant, and precise as pain. He who has paced for three decades the same slab of pavement smoking the same cigarette ruminating still on the same problem in his indoor voice; the boy who has waited for fifteen years under the intricate floral arrangements hanging from his mother's porch for his father to come home, waving at each passing car; constant flowers dead in a pile ceremoniously around lampposts—a sky, whole families, a white bicycle, dog, park, light, qualities of light, me.

Me. Weaving, ducking, swerving, light, full, light, full, finding everywhere evidence of breath. Head high, respiring, aspiring, high, rising. I am a family in the park. I belong. I own and am. My husband is possessive so I know he loves me. My bed is king-sized, my kingdom miniature. I sleep hard in the middle of it. My dreams are memorable and laundryless. I drink coffee and have opinions about it. I iron my clothes! I iron my *sheets*! Stacked, matching and clean. No, no, I pay someone to iron my clothes, my sheets, and more generously than average. I like to pretend that because we share an accident of birth, we have something in common. That because we have something in common, we have something in common. But I am blanched. (We barely have anything in common with ourselves.) Of course, I do not smoke cigarettes, marijuana, crack, anything. My smiles are not these grimaces, jilted by unknown history. My body is not desired only because of the roomy quality lent to it by congenital loss, which, though named by lovers as mystery, is only and again the unerotic and ordinary history of power. My cock knows when to be hard and for how long. All that enters is organic—lunch, tampons, limbs, organs and tongues selected carefully as summertime peaches, scented headily and fresh running down the chin, dripping neat as my reliable menses, my predictable disposals. Hair of itself has stopped growing on my legs, pubic mound, and underarms. I have a tidy desk. My house is many roomed with each room serving a single purpose. The entertaining rooms are full of different and unique friends whose hands are full of jars of chutneys and jams I have made from the fruits growing on the trees in my own garden that I tend to. Produce is produced productively, even the bees and I collaborate, the flowers—we are one! Hair, breath, thoughts and cash flow in ever lengthening straight lines. I am an American city, simple as a box. I have many non-acrylic sweaters. My shoes are waterproof, leather, stylish, my feet dry. There are no holes in them, my clothes, my sheets, my body. Hot rocks, wounds, pock marks, age.

Soon I am aglow once more, happy baby, industrious with the single-minded activity of self-preservation.

I was a universe, my own dromenon, perfect in my trance. My gates were regular, I knew the colors. Moonlit, I scaled the narrow ledge, exiting from one window and entering through the another. Storeys high, the honeysuckle, the cigarettes, could not reach me or, if I slipped, break my fall. No, better with limbs tucked in, away from the swamp's alligators, from the faces jeering at the window, away from concern's engulfing qualities, defining as they do the limits of love. Away from the onslaught of the door swinging open, catching me busy losing God again and in ferocious detail.

Though my questions were acute, stacking to make many knife-edged crystals aptly multiplying the light, when they saw I was alone they turned on me. I began to seek terror. Its consistency was holy. The long night abruptly folded into a tidy square into a flatness into a simple dot whose name was I. It became the wooden dolls, outfitted colorfully, to whom I made the secret declarations, swallowing them one by one with my head stuffed under the pillow. The unnatural fibres squirmed audibly, or was it the stuff inside my synthetic skull? I repeated the day's lessons into the mattress until everything around was hard as knowledge and slumber. I woke uniformed vomiting hearts and mushrooms. I communed with the thumb pressed along my tongue and named the animals what they already were. Nothing bored me more than astrology. Constellations embarrassed themselves.

Visions came, upright as school chairs and stiff as habits: every orifice a grave to be filled with dismembered limbs and garish genitals with their liquids. I got torpid, mud-like—out of me burst veins instead of flowers. Lust was an allergen.

Eyes closed behind the wheel I drifted, lights off, windows down, ten seconds, twenty, midnight, later, eyeliner, sneakers, taken by the muffled suburb. Phantoms of many sizes and opacities goaded and stroked me—a girl, sockless in winter aroused evenly by all things; a boy, so utterly sure, that he has written his name on everything.

I was small, but I was never a child. We are born on our knees —into guilt, work, emergency. The whole force and humiliation of puberty is every day.

I was ignorant, but honest; wise, but innocent. Beyond this I was my own sweet stone stoned nothing—since betrayed by trying to be something.

Now I am only a woman, raced, racing, stretched with objects and climbed into magnificent. Womby, ice cream, daybreak, lullaby.

Constant hostess, self-regulating temperatures. It is always room we are making, in time, the heart. What is the independence that for another is catastrophic? To accommodate another's little freedoms, I cut out my guts and lay them out in a mandala for the foxes, for the unmajestic birds of round here. Isn't compromise fun? Scarred, here is the character you always wanted.

Each pore a sinkhole and as sudden. I learn my place is only witness. My face slips from the world's face. Quaggy whiteness, cliff, terror. Scanning keenly for a signal the flitting motions of ears are arrested. Nostrils, little traitors, seal vengefully. For air, I gape but the jaw snaps up in its laughter. Cunt tightens. Lovers adore, beg, worship, queue up, fight each other. Tighter and smaller and tighter and smaller until it turns in on itself and seals completely. Asshole, urethra too, crystalline and shut. No waste will exit. It will fester inside until I am constipated and bursting, full of my own shit forever. I cannot have my own ingestions or excretions even. A pair of black eyes perch at the front, their pupils desperately dilated, observing, intelligent. Smooth, matte, above. This is the finest flesh. Paralysis preserves.

The insides are imperceptibly bruised from that which keeps battering the tissues and vitals trying to escape. Panic, a siren, spirit in ribbons.

(I am the tail of the lizard waiting for the body to rebuild itself onto me. I am not the lizard with a stumped tail, waiting for the rest to grow back.)

What remains is a flayed thing, sealed.

They know me. They know my insides. They know every expression on my face and what it means. They know the meaning of my silence. They know my body and its tastes, its gleanings and prescriptions, its fickle changes and doubts, its surliness. The skin, the fat, the muscle, the bone.

They ask. They opine. They care. They invite. They interrupt. They demand. They expect. They pry.

It strikes the back motivatingly to ensure no one falls behind.

Suddenly it eats at tables, wedded, and looks askance at the broken, the unhinged, wielding a screwdriver.

It is invasive.

It is conciliatory.

Friendship.

The familiar sits with identical hands, umbilically approving and disapproving of, assessing and analysing any new members. How will they flow with the factory's rhythms, what is the history of their tribe? Did they groom and till the earth nobly, did they trade in exoticisms, did they industrialize, did they heal or were they criminals? On which side of the king did they stand?

The clothing presses us down and in around the television, fire, which grows in size with every birth and death. The final judgement arrives after the men have gone and all the bras have been pulled from the sleeves and their tucked cups placed on the sofa's arm by the remotes. Our intimacy gets to be sharing discomfort and then sharing not-sharing it. Where will the new girl sit? I sigh along and weep and swipe but they do not know my underwear is crotchless, my potions herbal; they do not know that the red of my nails is only blood from my most recent kill. I save a seat beside me, hoping.

Why is it always the women queuing up at the pharmacy? Why is it never us who get to define who swallows what, whose senses are interrupting whose sanities?

Yes, even I have lovers. I get them from the Internet. I am successful because I communicate in a regular manner. I use only ordinary words and gestures. I am never alone on a Saturday night. I get every job I interview for.

When they arrive, we sit on the bed. They talk, I nod. They leave gaps I can ask questions into. It is a conversation. We are communicating. My lips are lacquered. We never eat the snacks. You can fuck a corpse but you can never feed it. When I open my mouth, it is never for a meal. They believe I am a good listener and they believe this is a quality of mine that they like—as much as they like my eyes say, or that because my only desire can be to be desired, I work hard and permit everything. And so not only listening but listening *well* becomes an important and therefore likeable characteristic, no, a rare quality, and so a valuable one—precious as loving a hand on my throat, squeezing. So they want to keep me, despite my poor body—plump, lovable, emaciated, shrill. It's the silence that arouses, that acrobatic sympathy.

Because they underestimated my intelligence, any shreds of it they see are elevated and worshipped as those idiots elevate and worship say, a piece of toast in which they believe they see the face of God, revealing only their own doubt, their own faithlessness. They spread out inside this awful feeling, mistaking for love the gap between their expectation of my stupidity and the reality of my aptitude. They expect me to be grateful for this insult, as if I could not see them happily realizing that

that handsome face in the department store window they accidentally pass by is actually their own.

I study their lips. I study their eyelids. I study the hairs glistening all over them. I smell them. I stare at their skin. I wonder whether or not they have souls. I wonder if the soul resides only in gesture. I wonder if gesture resides only in soullessness. I stare beyond their ears out of the window, leaping from it and landing silently on my toes, not looking up, not looking back, running beyond their flesh and mine, beyond the script, beyond the nullifying strokes. I smile. They sense its oddness and categorize it as my haunted quality then dare to play around in it.

The confused boy, who, poking with his foot the immobile animal at the water's edge, still has not discerned whether it is dead or deadly.

The mind goes, high on our theater.

I am extinguished, consenting.

I love letting go. I love being spontaneous. It's exclaimed on my profiles: "I love letting go! I love being spontaneous!"

My eyes clamp shut, flicker open, roll.

Where is my real choice?

They touch me and are not electrocuted. They feel my touch and survive it. When their faces break and crumple, spasm and sigh, I know I am not dead, but I also know that they could kill me. What pleasure will we choose when happiness is disentangled from relief, when freedom is disentangled from safety? Oh devotion! How it can fortify.

Too soon I am reformed, boundaried and stubborn, meat. It will take more. That nothing can touch me is my greatest asset and my most tragic weakness.

We part before the at-first serene, then undoubtedly more demanding, bucking and rearing of fondness might set in.

My hand is not fit to shake anyone's mother's, my smile too shrill to safely encounter siblings. Though I look the part, it is not me you want to take your nieces shopping.

When they go, I am relieved. I look in the mirror and watch the face change back into what it is. When they go, I am devastated. I look in the mirror and watch the face change back into what it is.

When they go, I launder and change the sheets, wash up the glasses, ashtrays and little bowls, dispose of the bottles, butts, food, and condoms, sweep the floor, air the room, vomit, shower, brush my teeth, take my pills, input my nutrition, and check my messages.

Because it will take more, I attend occasionally orgies organized by men so finely dressed that their misogyny gets outfitted as sophistication so sheer as to make critique seem undeniably paranoid. Gentlemanliness is conjured as the softest weapon, as though it only meant still believing in hats and rules about hats. Single girls half-price. My real friends were the dormice and the elephants, the wild and open-hearted; and our best intimacy was painting her nails, or wet shaving his face when he was sick but had to work regardless, or how letting ourselves be held was what strengthened our arms. At these events my hatred is perceived as aloofness, irresistibility. Doll. I sit at chairs pulled out, cross my poorly-stockinged legs, drink drinks brought to me eagerly, accept the bodies of others. They think my stained and sorry cotton underwear, my betrayed body is how I've chosen to look, as though I were catering to some kink-reality maid. They wonder at the natural cruelty of so weak a creature—not even empowered by lingerie. To seduce I do nothing, I simply ask for their watches and rings. They love feeling, without actually being, confused about who is at the top and who is at the bottom. I pick nimbly across strewn bodies to loot lucrative cloakrooms left trustingly unattended. I do not wonder if these bodies have souls—I wonder if they have cash. *Now* I am connected to everything.

For the seventy-five-minute bus ride home a man asks me, for each one of those seventy-five minutes, where the remote is, and I answer him each one of those seventy-five times, I don't know, I don't know, I don't know, seventy-five times. It is a conversation. His chapped feet stick out of decrepit brown sandals contorted by bunions shaped bulbously like the helium balloon adorned with a silver cross bound with pink and red bleeding roses tucked under his right arm and tied with a string to his belt loop.

Here I am, leaving in piles on each piss-stained seat small offerings from what I took: a fifty-pound note folded into an origami crane with a pseudo-sadist's signet ring tucked into its right wing and a creamy yellow rose petal at its tail; a twenty bent into a sail boat floating on a lawyer's designer silk cobalt tie arranged in waves with three torn petals for froth; two fifties constructed into an elegant box with inside it another two fifties folded into a smaller box with inside it a gold tooth ripped right from the gums of an almost recognizable politician and still bloody.

At his broken feet, I lay the rest.

How I love communicating! It is important to do so frequently, openly and honestly; to be responsible practically and emotionally for oneself and for the other; to be independent but not distant, interdependent but not codependent. When cohabiting—the economic imperative disguised as natural once more—household chores should be shared equally and often with cheer, and time and money budgeted lovingly. Be careful with your words—when to say I, when to say we. Be not overly concerned with the detachment of some limbs and organs: heads in laps, hands in hands, hearts in hands. Try to like each other's friends. Find activities you both enjoy. Try new cuisines. It is not enough to have a heart in common. Allow sexual acts to be playful, but never insincere. Suspect perversion. Suspect those who love solitude. Suspect asexuals. Support each other's dreams no matter how tenuous. Be tethered to the real earth even when joyfully unhinged. Be not overly concerned with the headlights sweeping across the bedroom window in the middle of the night, striping the room in bars. Enjoy inseparability's spacious trap. It is love's true trick, like pain's, to arouse a feeling of uniqueness: *no one has ever felt this way before*. It is exquisite—somewhere always bright as its first instance. Be easy with one another. Do not be afraid to cry. Allow occasional surliness. Know what to take personally. Do not monitor snacking habits. Perform romantic gestures. Navigate space and distance with finesse: remember, what is intimacy to one may be violence to another. Remember to laugh! It is ordinary as a chapter. Be comfortable: parents, children, siblings, lovers, friends, bugs, crazed, alone, together, good. Just relax!

It deforms:

these are not my smiles. These are not my words. These are not my little jokes. These are not my affectionate animal names. These are not my cute diminutives. I encourage them in your direction with one tongue but with another plead: please do not forget my name.

I do not want to be a cannibal. I do not want to be a dog. I do not want to be a virgin.

I have felt with others. I have lain supine in the sun. I have affectionately straightened out shower curtains.

I have adored timelessness and through it hallucinated eternity.

I have been saved. I have been worshipped. I have been a fat little god.

There were locks of hair, wax fingertips, shoulders cast in plaster and petal hanging from the corner of the bed.

In it there was no hunger, no rent, no work. They said it would eradicate hunger, rent, work.

It felt like a miracle.

When hunger, rent, work arrived, we tried to hold their heads down in the mud.

It felt like murder.

(But still, we love, including the hunger.)

When I loved, I loved like a mother, a child, a boy, a girl, a poet, a father, a pimp, an angel, a corpse, a baby, a dog, a cat, a breeze, a fire, a killer, a spy, a schoolgirl, an elephant, a lioness, a goat who ate everything, a pig who loved to fuck, a librarian, a gravedigger, a cop, a criminal, a fugitive, a mute, a monkey, a clown, a tightrope walker, an alien, an exile.

What will happen to the remains of our little dog? We followed it as far as possible to the shore and gathered in a circle around it. Eventually, one of us closed its eyes with our paw.

Is it my face or my master's plastering the local lampposts, ink running in the rain, missing?

Remember:

The beloved's respiratory system is no different to your own, or is as different to yours as to anybody else's.

The beloved comes from an ordinary modern building, with a contract and standard doors, selected for its proximity to the commuter belt.

The beloved comes from a place with mugs, a sibling, plugholes.

The beloved comes from a womb.

The beloved pisses directly into the water as though intending to wake you up.

The beloved is not the beloved by all other sentient creatures.

The beloved's misspelled words will be more loved than the words they refer to. The charm of each error will cause you to reconfigure correctness, then morality, then truth.

The beloved is separate and can, will, leave. Sick, you will bow down to the new buildings, grateful to their architects and councils for eradicating your old neighborhood's familiar places. You move further and further away. How now to quell every suburban hydrangea's blush?

The beloved feels betrayed when love does not conquer all. When you suggest that love is not what we arm ourselves *with*, but what we arm ourselves *for*, the beloved will express exasperation with your mere semantic games.

The beloved is too busy to see the gorgeousness of mundanity—how stillness comes from repetition, how everything is contained in stillness.

The beloved, when you weep, weeps too.

The beloved is often silent: do they want fucking, feeding, or leaving alone? Must you mince lithely around the wet edges of their life like a silverfish, or be right at its core essential as bread? The desperate interpretation of and search for signs in lieu of information or participation will be renamed "intuition."

The beloved decides when conversations begin and end.

Loving the beloved is the only protection against loving the beloved.

They will haunt you, will bring each tragic moment and each perfect one and press them singly into your throat for you to choke on whenever. This will be your new life: one of private and permanent mourning. Grief is only the length of time your mourning will be publicly tolerated after which only incorporation is possible.

Did you mistake the beloved for home? You wanted to belong, to know the rituals and sayings, to know from whom and where you come. But there are wiser things to dash yourself against and for, into and out of.

You will never be able to apologize to the beloved, to say the truest sorry for the moment you were seen in their freckled eye—and blinked.

Pain will run through you in straits as fat runs through meat, altering its shape, changing its color. What was red becomes a pallid string echoing in the flesh. It will stretch you as if on a loop, it will embroider upon your taut and breathless surface, working upon it daily. While you may bloom into an important decoration, you will never get to be the thread, the needle, the eye.

Loving the beloved is knowing. After loving the beloved nothing will be known.

Doubt will bring with it a certain agility, but it will never bend you towards the sun like that knowing did.

Doubt will bring with it the space between seeing and naming without which no new words will come.

Doubt will invent.

What remains is a flayed thing, porous.

I have a lot of people to thank.

To provoke a new feeling, or at least some shock, I know that my prescriptions must be altered. To alter my prescriptions in order to provoke a new feeling, or at least some shock, I must show commitment to improving, or proof of worsening: I promise that yes, I have only been eating the softest of oats and sucking on milk-soaked rusks as I peel back my arms to conceal the crescents dug in in distracted sequence revealing no code, no secret but chaos.

The application of six to twelve weeks of corrective therapies is promised by the state medical authorities, providing I can hold my position in the interim. Oxygen. In six to twelve weeks, enough will become known for this knowing to lead to improved conditions, to coax the body into responding to the sound of a bell. (We swim towards the bottom to check on the shiny penny, and swim back up without it.) But if this is life, and not only its edge, it is not improved conditions I want, but none at all. I half-remember once dreaming of the ability to imagine an unconditional kind of living. A flag is not humiliating because it is small, shredded and dirty, but because it is a flag. Where are the friends to burn it with? What is it to cringe at an arrangement of colors and cradle it also? What if there is only a fresh new me smirking on the other side? I hold our heads down so I can continue:

it confesses in a small hexagonal room, each wall of which is shared with another small hexagonal room whose walls are shared with other small hexagonal rooms and so on. Inside and strip-lit, floating in a white viscous material, its mouth opens before a pale stranger and emits the Anglo-Saxon psychological learned from everywhere. The whites of the stranger's eyes leak and spread into the iris's glimmering lapis, into the refractive cornea, breaking the delicate chambers and seeping out of his skull in sodden clusters slowly approaching with tentacular intent. It slurps its complementary yogurt (the probiotics!) as the stranger instructs in how to cope with and manage, how to cope with and manage these fears, the body, outside, circulation, even the cells mutating on the cervical walls. It can't wait to be eased into its new position. It rubs itself against the grainy neutral fabrics of the institutional furniture. It can't wait! He gives it acronyms to research, which, when they appear in searches later reveal only the initials of its own name. It learns conscientiously that whatever nebulous clumps of reactions, memories and desires can at that moment be dredged up or invented must be displayed levelly under neon to be cooked. It learns that everything has a private internal root and no history. (It is a conspiracy against mothers.) It is a yearning for unity that is suffered from, an umbilical desire to return to that uterine sanctity, which must not be sought with others—no friend or lover or amateur dramatics society or team sport can provide this; no nation, no party, no creamy bedtime. To reach maturity, he says, this unity must be sought with none other than the self—that constant stranger. It gets a personality and puts things in it.

Oh the thin line between sensitivity and weakness!

Brittle heart, is it metal?

It is possible to feel too thoroughly and thus be weighed down (an anchor, an anchor). To feel something for a long time is chided as dwelling on it or congratulated as commitment. It is important to accept loss and concentrate on building a new life.

Do I want to be a dog at the mercy?

No!

Do I want to be dogged?

No!

Between us, exactly in the center of the pine-effect table, so as not to assume anything, is a box of tissues whose exposed leaf ripples in the high-pressure area, which, when I duly weep and tears and snot come out of the personality, I refuse to reach for, though he nudges it softly towards me. I nudge it softly back—he ought to be weeping double my tears and will be in time.

Though it has been years since I've suffered them, I love to tell him in detail about the perils of menstruation and how the wind bends the boughs, about the impact of trauma to the cervical spine and of the birds' shadows shattering the earth's solidity. I extract pleasure from forcing him to maintain the neutrality of his features and expressions, as the leaking face and I weigh up the advantages and disadvantages of menstrual cups, suicide, gluten, friends. How are these evergreens possible? Why are the tomatoes anaemic here? I make five columns: fears, fantasies, realities, memories, desires. I write the same thing in each one. I wipe the face, consciously smearing the eyeliner, I blow the nose into the blouse sleeves which I wipe on the tulip cut skirt—its high waist forcing a good posture—of course I dress as a doll for these dates, my cheeks matte apples. Even my most intimate secretions may not be assimilated, they must be cast out. (But these are not the secretions he was hoping to hear about, with his tissue box, the hand sanitizer.) He keeps pressing me for pronouns.

Once, I worked myself up into such a torment of panic and agony, gulping and convulsing, that I vomited right there at his feet. Out came the corrupted tongue! Speaking me behind my back like that, whitening my alphabet. Where do all the dead letters go? It wriggled at the toes of his shoes as he sprung back. Finally, his face fell down and he leapt up for a nurse, a cleaner, a receptionist—some woman to clean up some woman. She took my hand in hers. I cleaned while she poured some water and caressed my neck. She filled the glass to the top because she knew I wouldn't spill. We kissed for some time. Sister, ecstasy.

After these sessions, I am so elated that all I can do is shop.

I make myself a god, just like he told me to.

I am lucky to finally have a straight story. Forward motion is possible. I can plan and plot. I am the paperwork. So long, dear circle, holding, breaking; dear spiral, tightening, widening . . . your groove had almost formed a cut; dear vortex, your crucial impossibility abandoned.

Armed with my new and easy to remember mottoes and a simple set of behavioral modifications I looked forward to a clean new I. Would it be the new me of my dreams? Goodbye to that pile of stripped flesh! Goodbye to those deranged senses! Will I be aligned, my weight distributed evenly between two feet? Will I finally be able to wear pleats? Will my kinks fall out? It is all a matter of perspective, easy to shift as a chair in a room—providing there is a room, a chair, the strength and space to move around and some remaining fissure in the spirit through which to imagine a new arrangement. I loop around the row of five circles, decreasing in size, showing the toes, for the first time, head on.

Everything is on the inside. I am only human. They turned me in on myself. They turned me on myself.

My education loved me most of all.

My face froze during the arrogance of school. They thought I was a mute as I pushed my fingers into the friendly surfaces, trying to break them.

We came to the desks as to the operating table, with the weapons of incision and invasion, excavation and archeology poised before those of understanding, their impossible questions. We lifted the lids and put our heads inside, banging until blood filled the inkwells and we wrote our dictation with it, concussed.

I wanted to be alongside, not always above or below, desperately ingesting and excreting the strength of my outline. I could negotiate with prepositions, not perspective.

I wrote a summer diary for my readers, leaving out the names of my family—those humiliating arrangements of letters that would unmask me. It was a double betrayal, revealing and concealing in turn the thief who I loved and the thief I could talk to. I appalled myself—disgusted again that pallor was an, the, an option. Who could I sleep beside? In which language could I dream?

Cold term starts with legs closed and hands in the air. My notebooks are clean and my ideas original. In rows the others wait for me to laminate their books, to quell their blisters with poise and a hot needle. Laborious but it gets me fed. My smile is devastating, my footnotes immaculate. The thick balm spreads, addictive. My conscientiousness ensures my survival. The stable ground enjoys the dapple of the fast-moving shadows of leaves. No landslides, no earthquakes, no sinkholes. No intangible burning core whose quick gases would kill us instantly. Mother weeps, having known perfection, its hot needles.

The eyes of my educator are muscular, enticingly, his speech, rhapsodic, flecking the mouth's corners surely. He has . . . charisma. His linens crumpled from reading, face, hair, breath, wife, child, whatever. Preoccupied with the coming world, each passerby imperceptible. The whites of his eyes leak and spread into the iris's gleaming lapis, into the refractive cornea, breaking the delicate chambers. With my hand in his he explains, as he sucks my fingers out one by one, that the city inside is imaginary and unpopulated. Over time it gets flattened—the powdered knuckles and streets, parades and gutters, each caramel sinew, the span, the top knuckle joint folding alone, vales and the feeling parts, bark, bone, nail, cuticle, every rabid lifeline, the pulse, those glorious local bowling alleys, the forgotten rivers running underneath, ludicrously blinking neon, rows, helixes, roofs, leaks. He tells me this pain is called learning. His words are solid and definite. They root, he feels the ground, walks its topographies confidently and maps them so his feeling may become knowledge, and ours, madness. He knows the trees and birds and people through naming them, he knows the history of tarmac, what roads ring the forest dendochronologically and where they lead. I take his thoughts and words and repeat them in phrases back to myself in the mirror until they go on me and change my shape. First my skin repels them and recoils, but as the sea draws away from the shore it drags the pebbles with it. Whatever growths come later, come later.

My true thinking begins with a languid explanation of my thoughtlessness. I take notes: dancing is purposeless motion, color is always compensatory, feeling is failure unless it is arousal or anger (that special arousal) and only in the factual texts might narrative approach truth. I learn to learn the way a bedside table witnesses. I understand the foolishness of poetic forms. I agree that no action is possible and relax into it. When I look into the eyes of those who might be or become loved and accurately see the figment I am proud. They sit weeping as I explain. I burn my books and notebooks. I do not write because each word contains at least five more and each five another five and each twenty-five another twenty-five and each six hundred and twenty-five another six hundred and twenty-five and on and on to the sea bed's border leaden and boisterous with life.

Bomb
disease
utterance
thorny hollow
slip

entrance
betrayal.
From the center, the veins compact, the cysts retreat, the bones cortical and cancellous gird.

Next I learn how to speak out loud:

it grows the enemy tongue, limber, which has this soporific thing it can rest to, but barbed too and boring right in at the tenderest points. It puts itself to sleep. The pressure beneath the surface is relieved, it barely feels the trephine. In the hands, it pats the circle of skull, pierces it and hangs it around its neck. The spirits leave and music too. This syntax reigns, organizedly. It wants to be specialized too, and with a good chair for the days. It buys an adjustable tilting footrest which bolsters its new perspective. Because of the cost, it knows its new perspective must be productive. Officially relaxed, it sorts all the words into right ones and wrong ones based on fashion and relevance. Outwardly, it revels in the obliteration. So few remain for use and anyway already amputated. It studies them on signs and in books with their mouths sewn shut, little hostages, limbless. Just another graveyard.

At colorless podiums, preachers whose only pleasure is power, who exclude from intelligence the senses, say how wrong so well and we applaud. They recruit us because they are envious, kneading our front brains until we too envy ourselves.

But at least it'll never be a fool in public again! (Its private destruction is only embarrassing for it.) Its gauche asides diminish into plastic sipping cups, into the winey comfort of afterwords; its knotty logics are cut, solved, and dismissed. At last it is admitted into the world of good taste, built upon what it excludes. It has within it room for bad taste, but sanctioned.

The final lesson is: fear humiliation most of all.

I too become the knowing and it helps me feel immortal. Yet when I dictate myself in the mirror I see that still my forehead is becoming lined, still my eyes are crinkling at their edges and my mouth, a puppet's, is marionetting to either side. My spine and boisterous feathers transform into the glinting minerals of knowledge. Constellations petrify. I pay him and leave.

Being this kind of mute looks like serenity but is like hearing a great party going on and never being able to find it. Always a boulder being rolled over the mouth. Body and voice may inform on me whenever so we ensure any movement is charming or necessary and any speech is an apology or occasionally a question.

When the gap to speak into is so small, it is inevitable that those talking into it will sound mad, trying to stuff everything in. Every speech act is the single suitcase for fleeing in an emergency. Their interjections are tolerated then pushed down with a finger. (Pressing a whole chile into the soil will eventually produce more chiles, grown out of the seeds exposed through rot.) Meanwhile, they scrabble around in the dirt wondering why they are dirty. Perhaps they are searching for rocks. Perhaps they want to speak only in a crowd.

One two walks the nice exterior with its flattering narrow palette. Bellicosity down, popularity up! My pheromone is malleability. In blunting intention I made a favorite smoothness—I can lie down in it! I like being this way, polished and to the side, too far to spot regurgitation, my decorativeness necessary. I was given the chance to be a screen. Watch my bland line unobsessed with animals or with the grass swaying one way and then the other or with how people in summertime sit out just being there.

A humming appliance is plugged into a power source in a wall. Behind the walls are the bodies of those who could not prove they were closing in. Lost, errant, owned. The bulb of the humming appliance is warming a patch into my educator's cheek, casting his profile, animated with the twitching of his increasingly agonized face, against the wall while we—our faces dark, our genitals loping, resistant—hold down his head.

My education taught me that everything is on the outside. I was never human! It turned me away from myself.

I learn more from the grandest swish of the fakest eyelashes at the drunkest bus stops in the deepest winters of the cruellest suburbs.

I learn more from the look in the eye of a friend as they turn from the mirror and ask me to shave the back of their head. I cup their lovely skull in my palms.

I learn more from watching the animal trust me as I pry dirt from the corners of her eyes with my fingernails.

I learn more from the uneven distribution of speech than from the content of it.

I learn more from the uneven distribution of certainty than from the safety of it.

I learn more from seven decades of repetition than from what is being repeated.

I learn more from kids on the train going: house house building site house track house no houses bottle bin building site McDonald's Lidl mouse house no house rat crane big bin bags plastic tree flower Argos park football tree dinosaur pond fence crane crane crane crane crane crane crane crane crane crane crane crane crane river KFC.

I know what heat is.

Writing almost remained, held by something below surrender and desire, below care and spite, refusing, despite its aphasic life, to die. A stone, a stone. Like most things I grew to love, I saw its cruelty immediately. But I saw also that its bright and definite cruelty was not at its core, in fact that it had no center at all and so could be met on an even plane—disorganized, adored, made stimulant—if not with the grace and cleanliness of an arrow arcing through air, then perhaps with the slow-gathering pace of scum, of lichen, of mold—of all that grows without a home, not even a home in writing.

I keep my head down only in search of stones. I get them from parks and neat gardens and around. I aim them at the cruel face on a billboard, a red light, lumpen luminous police.

I am only a sad vandal, gumming the eyes of the powerful—those who are simultaneously everybody, nobody and somebody—neutral, universal, unique.

Why may they have their eyes when we may not have our own?

I am lucky to work—at all and in so alluring a place, a place whose symmetries make me weep. It is all ordinary things, but exalted. A tap for example, can belong. Its functionality can be impeccable, its vocabulary sublime: threaded spindle, acorn head, body washer. Extending skywards and blooming from the earth, the pipes are nestled and cozy, owners, advancing in a buried network. They undergird, with a Biblical claim. They bring forth sure water streaming proudly and filtered through a historical density. Coolly standing in riveting machines and decanters it effervesces or doesn't, is touched with cucumber, lime, or isn't; is imported, Norwegian, Scottish, Fijian, or is soft and local. Even the rain is attended to, rounded up and guarded for the plants

which have never stuttered, or floundered internally for apical dominance. In darkness, they do not fear the sun's extinguishment, or question what it has dipped behind. It, in the morning, bends towards them, nuzzling to be needed. Their accommodations are deluxe and ancient—under the supple air, or warmly housed for centuries, massaged by one family's gaze. If it is climbing they want, relevant structures are assembled; if they prefer to chase along the earth, scuttling, a path is cleared. All conditions are possible, unconditionally. With athletic roots, or strategically frail ones, they handle the soil rightfully. Fateless, it is they that want to be eaten and plucked—folded into mouths and swallowed or displayed unavoidably as beauty. Their inflorescence is subliminally repeated in the decorative features of the wallpaper and the crockery verbose with announcements of events and occasions, weighted according to the diner's status, the napkins' edges frayed with charm and febrile for use. The soft furnishings of inside are

lit according to mood: the soul's interior can be adjusted or reflected: natural, romantic, opaque, normal, mournful, yellow, studious, white, warm, sharp, televisual, incidental, cinematic, soporific, party. Even dimness is resplendent when the texturing of what is between air and skin can be organized to surprise, to comfort, to be reliable, to be sexual. Skin can be believed in and disciplined so that velvet can be velvety and like sleep, marble can be sleek and for the morning, cotton can be innocent, silk erotic, wood truthful, plastic imperative and normal, terracotta suggestive and lemony, time flexible and loving. And so, extended, can the sanctioned body's fluctuations be monitored at a kitchen's floating island where everything is permitted to be felt: skin, hair, nails, bowels, uteruses, vaginas, anuses, eyeballs, urinary tracts, esophagi, tracheas, ear canals, nostrils, mouths, teeth, gums, cuticles, heels, penises, knuckles, nipples, livers, rectums, lungs, testicles, spinal cords, central nervous systems, ovaries, chakras, brains, skulls, bones, muscles, hearts, bladders, gall bladders, kidneys, stomachs and be cured of it and its associates: PMS, PMDD, fatigue, insomnia, bile, depression, stress, fertility, infertility, overproduction of mucus, cancer, alcoholism, dementia, pheromones, acne, fat, anxiety, thin, feeling sad in the morning, feeling sad in the afternoon, feeling sad just before bed, nightmares, psoriasis, too many feelings, numbness, anhedonia, low sex drive, insatiability, affluenza, puberty, menopause, menstruation, PCOS, constipation, mania, seeping, pimples, ingrown hairs, styes, cramp, flatulence, migraines, kidney stones, glaucoma, cataracts, warts, sores, verrucas, corns, bunions, stitch, night terrors, premature ejaculation, anorgasmia, asexuality, diarrhea, incontinence, heartbreak, rejection, appetite, deficit attention, desire and thus restored to that neutral, universal, unique that

balanced attentiveness that is held, cleaned, cooked, peeled, skinned, baked, fried, steamed, dusted, polished, piled, ordered, reordered, gathered, sown, counted, navigated, dusted beneath, taught, tutored, guided, advised, loved, nourished, wiped, washed, bathed, soothed, tended to, placated, inflated, bolstered, mentored, adored by pairs and pairs of hands and feet like mine struck and sodden in a tone ordinary

as milk which multiplies seductively, extracted from all non-human female mammals available for milking and every milkable plant: cows, goats, almonds, coconuts, sheep, buffalo, cashew nuts, rice. There is even milk without any of milk's qualities, forcing the word to buckle

back-like and lacerated, speechless under an unimaginable life roving an unimaginable home civilized by a decorative library revealing the hoax named reading, bare, petty, malleable

if

I am, I am

curving always up towards opulent certainty: sure, I'd love to, that sounds like a good idea. I teach what suits the ruling class, I am a servant of the nobility. I try as conscientiously as ever to be the product of power multiplied by need. If my employer requires a burnished gold color with giant acorns at either end, then I am a burnished gold color with giant acorns at either end; or a made to measure support for a rare ammonite tightly coiled on a single plane to rest seriously upon; or whatever will remove the wax of a good time stylishly coating the heron candlesticks; or where the ornamental Chinese plate whose gold and orange dragons and minute lotus flowers and pink pagodas were painted elaborately with a single-bristled brush that is my ashtray went; or the charm of a contextless fez; or polish for the oxidizing steel of an ornamental key to nowhere; or the bold geometries of kilim. My folds are abundant as velvet falling lushly and gathering in excess on the floor and still continuing to fall.

My name is only the name for those who do as I do—we heard this doing was its consequence and natural. I change my name to her pronunciation of it. Now I can speak without mumbling, stuttering. My employer gives me a voice, words, a face and body, their possible expressions and ranges of motion. In her push-up bra, my form and employer are happier. Here I adore being myself, finally glowing with application. I smile at her animals and pet them with sharp pencils, poisoning them a little daily. Under the table I crouch at the child's feet in my lurid costume stuffing numbers into numbers. On the day of leftovers, the excess keeps dangling over the edge, eyes unmet, a sheet of hair, the popping head of a governess, the decimal infinitely recurring and getting swept into pristine invoices. I reach in after the child's crumpled face but comprehension is lost. When it weeps, I stroke its head, when it draws a line of triangles called family, I add the curlicue of smoke over the chimney curving always upwards as a smile

expands the chest which once felt love and asks now if love is only a desire for recognition, then is this it? It is a kind of ardor yet when I turn to my task and feel my boss's satisfaction searing into my hunched back, when I turn coyly over my shoulder, carefully dissecting a word and scraping its parts into the relevant bins, and still she is there, watching me, my irrelevant authenticity. She looks fondly too at the charmingly chintzy teacup chipped just so and plugged with geraniums resting on the least nice guest bathroom's sink; at the early works of Young British Artists she has wisely selected, purchased, and displayed; at her garden blooming with the blood-black tulips

I suggested she plant. I want to be as valuable, to adorn the walls, rational as advertising and as looked at. What reduction will I dream of next? What would she see but herself? What would I recognize but her? We lock eyes and my waist slims. She touches my shoulder and I am right as every pronounced T.

When she is out and I am bathing secretly in her tub I long for sickness to strike in order to force an invitation to sleep in her home. It would take two cooperating hands to pull the heavy curtains across the rolling greenness beyond the great windows through which would peek the real sun in slivers apt as poems come morning. My toes pretty in her bed, my fingertips suddenly quaint and agile, my eyelids light and thin, their blue veins imperceptibly nudged awake. I am so myself I can hardly feel it. I feel instead the bath's rolling top under my warm palms as I lower myself in, my reflection in the golden tap ripples and is flattered into a narrow torso and larger breasts, a proud plump belly, a small nose, bigger eyes, even elongating and straightening my hair. The water works to lift my breasts into perfect rounds peeping out of the water milky with organic products, almost edible, or, in fact, edible, but perhaps inducing sickness—so I try. I dip and scoop body scrub, figs and almonds, cocoa butter and astringent lemon to tighten the pores, I swallow and keep it down. I add conditioner, coconut-based, and taste the bathwater in sips. Clean and churning in my ordinary clothes she finds me cradling the toilet bowl, vomiting really—well-scented capillaries on my cheekbones popping customarily, the sweet patches no lovers kiss no more. Bound to a bed, my forehead acknowledged, a compress, a bowl of soup on a perfectly slanted trayble. To not miss a moment, I sleep with my eyes open and the curtains too on this loveliest night of fiction. The moon progresses in an arc reflected in the long neck of the heavy spoon and my liver exhales. She cures,

even making a charity with her artist friends to help poor Arab children so she has no time to do her hair which is gathered in expensive carelessness drifting in rays around her face or in a ponytail swinging so merrily it turns almost 360-degrees behind her skull, a turbine, genetic, reflecting light generously unlike mine absorbent, greedy, hers inspires, motivates—I'd cry, I'd kill for it. Standing before her dressing table, no, sitting, because her dressing table has a seat, and the seat has a cushion, and the cushion has flowers, and the flowers bud and bloom and die and bud and bloom and die, she sits in the same position and with the same posture, familial, lovely, as her mother sat at her identical but slightly larger dressing table, and as her daughter sits at her identical but slightly smaller dressing table. At these tables, and in unison, they pick up their wooden-handled soft-bristled brushes, meet their own eyes and each other's eyes and brush. Oh how easily it slips through! There is no resistance, no entanglement, no tearing—only smooth unchanging beauty more powerful than mouths or cunts, eyes or tongues; more powerful than the arrangement of features on a face; more powerful than legs or breasts. And we squat ironing our ears flat, we crouch over the hairdryer eradicating baby hair with a singe, pulling our hairlines into tents so hard that our eyelids distort and come away so the bright white eyeball's separateness is remembered with a gasp. We never swim, never feel being entirely in water. The mellow throb of hair against the back gives them always a rhythm to walk to, always someone to walk with, sometimes it is me

who is her friend. What is a modern friend but an approximate human with elbows to lean on and discuss death with in the kitchen? I pretend I still menstruate as we consider the row of supplements hovering beside our golden tea which levitates in silken pyramids, its components stratospherically uncommon and sipped down mindfully, her humanity glowing as mine is tapped and drained, naked lymph. A game is being played: every time she says natural cycle I try through the hole in my pocket to catch a stray hair on my thigh and pull. She drinks it hot, it scalds me but I keep up. (My organs are superfluous.) Her favorite bit is to pretend that because we share an accident of birth we have something in common. That because we have something in common, we have something in common. I manage occasionally to grip the tip of a fine hair and pull without pinching my flesh. (As a child I trained myself to stop wincing.) The patch below my right thigh pocket is studded with angry red lumps. She tells me she is so glad she's found me, that all her friends want one just like me. See—my education kept its promises. Now I am a cool spacious room,

I am a dead bluebird, suicided against the conservatory glass, scooped up kindly and dropped sorrowfully outside. I am the blood and feathers of the dead bluebird stuck haphazardly to the front paws of the ginger tom licking his chops and stalking grandly through the cool spacious room. I am today's lesson about death. To soften the blow, I wear ruching which is echoed in the crimps gathering around the stamen where the petals of the calico flower barrette in my immobile hair gather and splay in an approximation of the aphrodisiacal orange blossom whose scent I've used behind my knees and ears just enough to suggestively alter the air. My stubbed nails are pomegranate pink and I sucked a spoonful of honey just before I arranged myself like this, knowing exactly the moment the husband will enter with his globed back, his universe, his narrow gait, and want to eat me, to dissect me and decide the names of my new edges and what puppets will be their kings. To exist he must cast and trawl and drain, chase and maim and sever. He does not want me to remind him that the food in our mouths is the starvation of others—my sisters, my brothers, that my yes is the silenced no of another. Honey-breathed I mutter a song in a language he does not know in a melody he could never comprehend which circulates in me, buried. Later perhaps he will click into a different subcategory on RedTube, where eyelids are heavy with kohl and the elaborate hips are scored to some imitative microtonal song. Relaxing against the doorframe loosening his tie, a sitcom, he sees me. He does not want me to seduce him, he wants me to provoke him. He does not want to possess me, he wants to be changed through contact with me. A contact that will only add more him to him.

Is it an ounce of his solidity I want? To wake up the same every morning only recognizing myself more over time, to get to be a fat everywhere and yet rooted and with a tartan all of my own? For my sentimental remembrances to be part of my loveable qualities and a shared experience too, not excoriated, to not be from somebody else's memory of a place? To be listened to as if I contain some germ, some origin, like I decided language too? Do I want to live inside his private omniscience also? Is it warm inside? Does it burn? Could it?

Could I throw my head back with the other birds perching on the high edge of the shiny enclosure and sing? Would that be life?

Or is it to walk at noon with others, after she has pressed a five-pound note into my palm for lunch and I have knelt to kiss her ring in gratitude, to the supermarket under my big person crown? Oh compassionate rocket, gem baby, succulent heirloom rows, at once a thirst and its quenching, juice redeems, a desert, the sea, let me swim for hours, mango, coconut, pineapple, papaya—is this paradise? Is this unoccupied space? Is this the creamy squish of balance? Why then are the shelf stackers constructing pyres and in the aisles smashing their heads against the freezer cases competitively? Solitary and lightly-salted everyone quick heeled for punctual pay. Please let tonight not be too argumentative and sad to press against with the people and little animals we call home—that slender rocky dimension speciously named, tight and squeamish as veins.

We gesture wildly at the surface of lunches and wait to be selected and pried open—how else will our insides get different? I stand harder to better feel the movements of others all around, the breaths and gusts and mutterings of little swifts and soon I am in the sky, one of them, one of hundreds and long-winged too, soaring across the clouds, our shadows trailing us as we pick together one high roof over there to perch on, arching and dipping and patterning the phlegm-constellated pavement, the triangle of green, the rainbow-flagged steam baths, the kids spilling out of the chip shop, the green lights glowing feverishly over the area's now esteemable properties, the unending sorrow that is the only continuous thing, the deranging flashbacks of all that was lost and keeps getting loster, a solitary strutting cat, nests stolen and souped, the ravaging comprehension of what regret is, the dead fox in the road and we pick one high roof to approach and as we do our shadows break sharply at the right angle between ground and building and scan rapidly up the wall studding it with shaded patches which from inside must create flashes—we are spectacular, we land effortlessly. To celebrate we throw our heads back and sing and so on the days when she presses a five-pound note into my palm for lunch I don't eat any food but scrunch the money up and eat that instead.

Even in my fantasies the lover rips off their face to reveal the lipless one of my enemy. Even in my fantasies I cannot touch the lover's flesh until we have discussed the squirming medical histories of our genitals. Now my fantasies are only of fantasies shimmering below the water's surface is a swaying kaleidoscopic coral alive with fan-tailed shoals of easy fishes who flash together as a beat and one by one in staccato like the unlucky guppy with its ornamental vermilion and black dorsal fin which is now clutched by the fan of its striated tail between the pomegranate pink tips of my fingers and wriggles and gasps against the air. The proximity of warm shades pleases me and this being pleased ripples disarmingly through my body in synchronicity with the unfortunate rainbow fish's final gulping torsion. Scooped from the vast aquarium that rests on the antique mahogany sideboard in the library, the dead guppy, finally a definite article too, is the key component to my irrelevant trick—the latest in a string of weak sabotages which never extend (I dream alone) from mild irritation to voracious infection.

I slip its body and those of its friends into the hem of the velvet curtain stretching across the bay windows of the same room and wait. Expanding through every coiling twist of all the house's drains and U-bends are vicious products hauled and poured to eradicate the mysterious odor spreading steadily. With appropriate facial expressions I make passive speeches detailing the effect of such chemicals on our environment, our sea life, on nature's gormless insistence—see, I am a tender-hearted, environmentally conscious, eminently employable person. I say "our" so they, in noticing they have noticed "our's" equalizing gesture, feel only more acutely the difference between us. (I am learning how to use language, see, how to force words to buckle.) My nature is a little weed growing between the cracked stones of a windowsill, or some mold behind that sink, blooming under my encouragement.

More noses are summoned to locate the smell, things are overturned, a minute and delightful chaos foments but too soon fizzes over into unexpected camaraderie: they are enlivened by the conundrum, they are united under it. Oh community! I fail. Quickly, I remove the guppies, swallow the rotting evidence and suggest the curtains be sent to the cleaners. Any lingering energies are neutralized. That tree in their garden is still older than the place I am from. I still know their genealogy better than I know my own. I still know even the names of their houses, dogs, horses, wives, ex-wives, cousins, schools, companies, medications and hereditary diseases. The angles in a triangle still equate to 180-degrees. But if I am

I am part of their world, this world, hairballs and the cats that retch them, this smell, autumn's fetid mulch, the floating waste of sewers, the pavement's hocked mucus, all that is spat out by disgusted creatures, that which will become fuel and be burnt, that which burns, the carcasses of dead pets, spring-pink cherry blossoms swirling, each pigeon's shit adorning each mansion's windows, the arm of the woman stretching around the grand window's edge to scrub thoroughly away at it, her other hand resting on the interior window's sill for balance, I am the shit itself being slowly but evenly scrubbed away and falling in specks and flakes to the sill or the ground, parts of it sticking to the rag which is not a rag but a pale-blue microfiber ultra-absorbent ultra-strong cotton cloth that came in a pack of three for £10.99 from an online delivery from a luxury supermarket from a warehouse in Hatfield from a factory in India from the cotton of the cotton fields of Maharashta picked and decontaminated manually before being spun by the blistered hands of masked suicidal pickers and which, upon washing after use, will shed itself in microfibrous granules and eventually be deposited into the great plasticisation of oceans. *Now* I am connected to everything. As long as I scheme alone my biggest scheme will remain only a paltry one of being for one thrilling moment the waste of vermin coursing momentously through the cool air as if with intention but only ever accidental, a creature

with a head at either end of its eight-legged body, felt and lurid, stands on my broken heater touched by the light from my surroundings lending it a fearsomeness it does not have when it is clutched as a favorite toy between the paws of the employer's child. To what body it refers I do not know and yet I pierce its eyes with pins and stop its nostrils with needles. Still, it is replaced by three new playthings and the child advances from prince to king. Impotent now, I dispose of it.

I fail. So I ensure to eat doubly at their table next time and only of the most expensive foods regardless of my desire for them. What appetite I do have is for the violently bland—unsalted boiled potatoes, blue jeans, white bread—but nothing tastes better than eating out of spite. I eat when I'm full and fast when I'm hungry. I feast at their table gorging myself long after they have stopped, forcing them to wait politely concealing their disgust until I have finished every available morsel of every available dish including the bones

covered in flesh covered in hair which for weeks I do not touch. Triumph of fuzz and mop. Horrified, the employers move around me as though *now* I am a monster, as though

now I am the skull-adorned moth imitating the queen bee's brood-stilling squeak while I fly towards the nectar amidst the nest of bees and drink, careful not to drown

in my reflection glimmering at me finally, echoing from my dressing table mirror as the blood-black tulips' stems are cut by the scissors in my hands at recommended diagonals and arranged emotionally in one of my great crystal vases

a pharmaceutical severing of the tops and bottoms of sensations makes them short range and manageable, malleable, selectively not re-uptaken and so flashing back and forth between two flat shiny surfaces bouncing curls landing now in a ring around the dressing table's cushioned floral budding blooming seat from which nothing will grow, despite the vitality of blood dripping from my just-pierced ears studded with handsome diamonds, bloody heirlooms, matching the necklaces and bracelets spiralling around my limbs and falling in anaemic seduction between my breasts upheld in my half-empty mauve lace bra and matching knickers

which I bend into my exquisite mouth, lined and painted classic red with a brush intended only for this color and purpose, as I masturbate on my sumptuous bed with one of my favorite dildos—how could there be desire for skin on skin? My jewellery slips poetically over my body, cool and surprising, refining me as it flows over me and tangles, shorn hairs dusting my body, reds staining the sheets—I am focused, I study my face in the photograph of me on my bedside table pinioned into a wedding gown each arm held by a man and as I come my eyes turn blue.

Now may I formally disturb your space? I dress for the occasion in one of my husband's suits, too close over the hips and pooling around the ankles need altering so I slice off their bottoms and conceal the gaping waist with the suit jacket's cool slide over my my skin which feels acutely given its frequent micro-derma-abrasions. I am getting younger—

it is time that is my covert partner. I can extend it backwards and put my hand in to get proof for anything because I make the law and its language, the language and its laws. I can pause it and live in the moment because it is I who designates when action should commence. I can even propel it forwards and secure the future because that is the thing I trade in. I can run it over my veins and put a stop to everything. It is a blade capable of slicing—connections and arteries or the littler capillaries coursing obliviously underneath, blushed and arousing, each one a seam bridging dumb flesh to relentless flesh, fringed with threads loose and to be snipped off with

the pair of gleaming scissors open on my dressing table alongside tufts splayed in the foreground in high definition, black petals plushly forming the background, the lavender silicone dildo strewn amongst them and the mauve of the bra escaping the blazer whose shoulders are speckled now with burst droplets of blood from my earlobes, each one reflecting the entire scene in its little orb intricate as the red filaments tendrilling the pair of glassy blue eyes now rolling in my palm. The finest accoutrements of my being are positioned meaningfully for my portrait, captured in a simple photograph of a reflection and sent immediately to myself

my neutral, universal, unique self

tosses the remains of its hair like her, leans casually or with a flourish

against her objects, does her smile, perfects her laugh, her walk, the
length of her limbs and eyelashes, allows her vocables to flash along
and ridge the tongue garbling it with the same syllables chiselled onto
the pediments of the city's finest institutions, teaching it to use the
idioms with total confidence, knowing their bloody roots and loving
them, the parallel wounds they make

against the chest under the scissors' tip along the wrists in a warm
cut left to bleed in her almond milk bath youth soaks away a smooth
blade plunging into the chest searching for if heart remains and whose
but the veins repel the cut and the bones scoff at the wan attempts at
puncture prone against the tiles a common body normal as dirt lump
studded blood stubborn remains screeching in the veins cells diverting
and rearranging as iron filings reveal the field around a magnet
repellent pinpricked solar plexus blooming no blood no springs
no gushes dig fail no release no oblivion no inside no outside only
ineptitude the deviating hand the disobedient mass

whose blood is this even? Does it belong to the walker whose
lovely thigh I long ago attached myself to and have since been
feeding off? Am I a tick? My parts are animal and engorged. What
dormant disease can I offer? I could be a tick, living on the snuggest
shrug of a dog's coat. I could be the dog! Its bite. Begging in the
smallest hours for a leash. I could be grass, a blade, a leaf, one of
many, swaying, trampled, mown, pissed on, growing, idly picked,

crushed under wheels or boots, an allergen, decorative, comfortable, suburban, precious, conciliatory, green. Was it my leg? What lies latent in my cells? Inherited, contracted, congealed—the blood of other creatures—a parent, a parent's parent, each lover's lovers, labor, dust, semen. Vibration. Able to spread and destroy particularly or, resonant, able to inspire. Whose story is this? What is the object of this sentence? The subject? A life, a koan. Whose flesh this lump that refuses, whose thudding embarrassment? My portrait is so good I mistake my limbs for leaves and eat myself.

Is this finally sympathy? Or only caricature? Is it verisimilitude or catabolism?

Here I am! I share many fictions with humans:
my arms! My legs!
Observe my pilfered barrettes, how my hairs come down.
I did what it took. Will I count out there?
I laid myself very carefully on top—why then this intolerable remnant?
Ash and mucus, sweat.
What is this stuff still leaking out that I stuff back in with my fists?
Gross residue.
I went to school for so long. My bioloquism was terrible.
A shadow only follows, like the world's dark past,
primed, keen and variously armed.

Big silence for history.
Keep spitting in the dark for water to drink or drown.
What compression has occurred or what expansion?
The edges are frayed betrayers,
my hands are filling with excess—
here freckle and burn, lowly pimple, there down and wire, inversion and shallow pit.
Why must I have her eyes, here, rolling in my palm, skull, when I cannot have my own?
Why must I have this stone, here, sitting in my palm, skull?
Conscious, conscious.
Is this molasses underfoot or concrete?
We have been walking for some time.
The surroundings have altered dramatically.
Young tongue spurts out of the head beneath our shoe.
Now I might hear.
What does the yeast say?
Speech is saliva, stuttering, unsayable.
I line the streets with metals, with diamonds, wrap chains in the boughs, ring the thorns with gold, adorn coiled peaks of turds with single pearls, stuff precious stones between the pavings—but why are my organs out?

Liver swings glistening brown along the air
numb muscle heart got the easiest job in the factory

guts these ropes writhe infected beyond the body for hours after death
exhausted and siamese the kidneys float behind
membranes sheer garnet filters
uterus half-fecund bulges and mocks
throat sewer of tubes
tarry lungs
gorgeous bronchials collapsing and flattening to a gulping ocean
secretive pancreas housing crucial ducts
piss gutters breaching
bladder swole
slick twist of ileum strictly surveilled
more wet gut bits squirm spasm knot
most central disturbance
long pleat of cunt working
an alleyway storage solution
delicate cervix waning
squatting rectum ill disordered torn worshipped
skin gapes ignorant.

Is that my face or my double's?
It has my real mind.
I reach and it goes—my hand dissolved into the spongy beyond.
Its smirk a coil lampooning the mouth.
That stone, that stone.
Preposition is error: no inside, no outside.

Already entranced, thronged with fine edges
but unable to show up to nothing,
only vapid meat bound tight enough to mistake for s/kin, congealed
down to the bone
rushing the space with filling, with noise
hollow valley droughting asking
is this rain upon me?
Is this sunshine or mosquito?
Cement
repulsion
osmosis
starvation—
compelled only to charge in as a liquid
to an empty breathing space,
to join, design, widen the pen,
to squeeze the circle into the pouting dot of order—

For protection: stories, spaces, identicals, lovers bound, friends expelled, stacked against the image which beats. Essence conjured and deployed in emergency from within and by force from without; conjured and deployed to the edge of itself and then halting, as if before a ravine, seeing only abyss and not the stream which formed it nor the space it describes and its possibility—the leap, your own emergency.

This is safety, a sort of cleanliness. The adored tribe is also a racket—a fiction, particular and necessary, temporary. This is privacy, the cute superiority of love. What of love not in contradiction with solitude, and solitude not in contradiction with being together—not only a recovery from hate, stoned and furious insomniacs. This is escape, little inbred police called friendship, text accessory, unwilling enemy.

Now look! Here comes the fat hug of belonging—the president's apology, the great renaming, a rehabilitation, the padded recognition, updated census categories, the very specialness, the folding in, the guilt assuaged, a new edge to cut our distance on, politely barbed to bleed without complaint, compliant.

Inferiority lifted loves a gag it gets to pick itself, sidling in the cool side to marry breed work vote rule die. Debt, like gratitude, gets eternal. Here tongues are bleached clean in a row, chalk outlines finally drawn. We puff out our chests and enforce hospitality, weaken knees for the feast. We eat at last, faced and broad with excitement—but find the orange dry and lifeless, the date shrivelled and hard. Action, elusive flint— doubtful, mercurial, lazy—could quell the embrace. The circumference meets its own end and designates a new region, taking with it the town's well

oh thirst

upon thirst

congeals into brutality

so commonplace as to appear, become, essential, and each attempt at movement justifies the use of more rope—

no heat, no grace, no bread.

Turning this way, turning that, either way we get defaced in both directions. Where will I look if not always over our shoulder? The face that isn't turns to blood which rolls out like a tongue eventually and as lustful. It dictates the actions—so hot it must be true. It goes in a circle tightening because it does not satisfy or nourish. But what delicious thing should be avoided and why? Health is an enchanting luxury. Would success make torturers of us too? Would our faces get stuck in their gorgeous new glee? Mercy slopes archaic. Is bloodthirstiness housework too? What house, whose blood is being let? Wrong murder again. I want to dream more than a murderer's dream, live more than a murderer's life.

So the face turns back, relieved, already imagining smelling the imagined smell conjured in the exiled mind of the child of an exiled man with no memory. No sewers, no hot tar, no corpses. But whose smell is this even its to smell? And what can I know, lapping clean water on this great island, molesting my little flesh to expand into a bursting, feeling only someone else's feeling? Citizen, vile categorizer, in memoriam. What arrogance, gilded and fed. Or is this pity? No, envy. No. Yes. No.

Oh ambit claim. I've never been home in the first place, stranger.

Behind their curtain, laughter—our search, our circle, turning in a cage, decorating the bars, sliding images of our ancestors—rapists, lovers, fighters too, slaves and traders, traitors, organizers, poets—between the mirror and its frame, already tilling and reaping, arrows poised.

We study the wrong memory. We turn away, again, away, again, away—pervert. We burrow down, steadfast, learning the boiling earth.

What can I recall without memory? Only a melancholy tone—pat and shallow, not much but a fragrant impression. You eat oranges like your grandmother unknown. There is no use in weeping. How the enamel corrodes. This is not my key to nothing but I try to bear it lovingly. Still, it is impossible to believe in.

I did not know how to take control of a memory's memory. Could I be slight enough to listen and still enough to see? All their stories are garbled far away from sense and further yet from poetry. A broken story is not a poem. A story that cannot exist but wants to is not a story. Or, theirs are the words that must not be incorporated—goiters, or: how to prevent resting inside a correction.

Here the family objects are somewhere in a chest, a story, intact and novel. But we, we have these permanent votives burning. They rely on our amnesia. Ours is the arduous ardor of remembering not to forget, or: learning. Form.

I won't walk back the same way I came. I won't give up the names of my mothers or italicize the food we eat. I won't write the story that keeps us in our places, peered at sensitively from the radio and awarded. I won't find a home in the end.

I have no card to play. Both sides of it are blank. I'm no hunter. I dig down. We see others. There are tunnels under the world and out of it. Portals.

I sweep this ground and wash it. I light a candle. I sweep *this* ground and wash it. I light a candle.

To encourage steely climbers, a way to scale a wall, we must keep the graves clean. But not for love or pride. I do not clean the dirt from under my nails after I plant the jasmine, the bougainvillea, the geranium. When I smell them, it is the smell under or above the one I know so well, that keeps me alive.

I turn towards, I turn away, perverse, already moving, face twisted by our own design, by the violence that made it, its hewn expression, pressing forward still—pissed on, a place to stick a flag.

What is behind my punctured throat? Is it only he, his chemical, or is something crowning there, hidden and hale? Trained upon full nothing, beaming, a polestar. Nerve, sensing.

In this crucible we may be more than forgery.
Hierarchies of interest.
Symptoms of narrative.
Specific deformations.
Damaged particulars.
Audacious, flexible
young supplicant's stupid head fell off
we sprung out headless
feeling the whole world from this hole in my neck
nerves hanging out
copper veins and cables sparking and puking
disgust disgust
guts out and feeling, pulsing, pulsating, squirming and sick, sensitive
tentacle, leading no way out
a face without bones
defaced
whose
no garden poem either, no skeleton, no ghost, no haunting, no answer,
no sorrow, no pride, no name . . . category error
: monster—singing the saddest song of the saddest choir who sing
songless despite the infinite night: here we are!
Tongue-tied and maimed
dreamless, the world's ugliest sister, insomniac, runaway
death march dancing to livid vibration
party without celebration

lament without dirge
against itself, for itself, with nothing but itself
perv
this is proof not sentiment
resonant beyond infection
what can a face do face down?
Listen:

Dawn.
Crouching over. Airless. Light—caustic, in oblongs, in ribs, panels, between and in through skeins announcing the bones. No temperature. Not exactly. But wet, of fog. Pressing. Ozonic odor, spring. Soily mouth, lids, grit under gums, nails and in cavities, coating claw, beak and plume, tuft ripped, appalling. A sickness over the city, squatting greenly, teeth out, keen, moving with slow ease, certainty, sharpening on us, ever florescing, toning the sky lime and bile, acid hue in ribbons sprawls tentacularly, into between the ravines of buildings frail or permanent, or gutted, or fresh, fresher without, burned, empty, flung; snaking round hard temples, glass, denouncing the sour clouds, leaking over heaths, over marshes, teal, saturating slim chimneys, brick, asphalt, concrete, tile; forming and entering chapped pores, knuckles of invisibles, seeping up from bowels to spiral over coiled fox shit, dappled palest pink in new blossom, ankles, calves, muzzle, straw, hound's nostril gaping, rabid. Breaths pinioned singly to white grass, white earth, withering a blade and returning, withering a blade and returning. At acute angles metals lean, shading corners flat, surface, pinch, gleam, bright burning mouth, broken glass lining perimeter walls, shred, heal, heel. Arches hollowed for greased haunches hung in glistening gyration, flesh fucked in good pools, water filling lungs till death as puberty disguised makes even this light hired. Harried locals' invisible face, homeless, undeserving of parks, rust in rivers dripping down new structures, clumping in clumps at the bottom corners is how time passes now—with its bones out, parched

and jealous. At even the sky eyes open competitively, enough blue enough—

Muscle threads humid city   walking nerve unpaid   rabid gesture
beak open   squalling   for big bird's regurgitation   ravenous for
its song   to listen with the whole flesh!   oh sensible still born
stubborn still   lucid despite interruption   boils acne rot lavender
wrong murder again   half sorry only   unfamiliar dear
here whinging hungry ever forgiving
again the years of tasselled slip on loafers and blouses
which bow at the neck!
no one has loafed in my lifetime
no motion has been purposeless
fear of color   pleasure   beaten out   worn with pride
new insistence on muted tones: the mannequin hand
honest hair   demure shapeless wartime pattern
efficient hell in common
found kneeling head open at the bare feet of a butterfly
with the bus stop   old women smoking laughing
bless the bloody forehead   for having tried escape   smoke blue
lycra diamante appliqué stretch denim cheap lamé floral
spring is beautiful on the A23!
plastic bags around the ankles   fragile wings   inedible fruit
debris inside
vine stalk sticker core
is this the underworld?
is this paradise?
see   elaborate sunset palm fanning across toenail's scene

coolest green   flamingo pink   mellow above the piss vomit
glass shit bones   barefoot on heels   toes separated
stretched up for cover   walking along
Norwood High Street
is this life or its edge?
outside KFC
mask boy window
glass hit repeatedly
forehead hit weight
whole scrawn behind
hit   weakening   hit   blood beginning on head   hit   glass
concerning around   hit   clusters of nerves ignite   hit
rush   hit   crack   hit   safety shatter fist shoved through
star   stretching to open car door   victory spit against words'
constant plea constant question
: tell me who I am
instead:
here I am illegible
(get ready for the big hairs down below   taken aside   told
low toned with inside brains   there was a letter from school
blood will come)
mucousy albumen in long veins wiped along the floral
back   where infants are plumped watered amongst cushions
machines function well   burn warmly   are gathered around
tradition holds a throttle   little vandalisms daubed

all behind and under   clogged head spaceless head
stuffed saturated   in farmyard   tones minor but
steady refusal   map of intrepid animal   sick
of carrion worship
of every tear having to have a reason
of every hat a head
of every man a woman

—here is a place where
something didn't happen)

Moorland Road in the 2000s

a woman   skirt gathered in lap   shitting into the gutter
teeth beaming skywards   first blossom coming down
lichen   needles   condoms   coke cans   graffiti   huffed
aerosols   flowering lilac weeds   cracks   walkways   passages
alleyways   before or after school or during it   loitering lip-
glossed   knowing the curve of neck and shoulder are only to cradle a
telephone
cigarette passes between lively behind the world
taking root radical   swing limbs around   desperate
customization torn   hitched hiked   hands clasped
cheeks cupped kissed   admiration hatred bouncing
between   widening the walls   boyfriend father brother
pity hate   hearts flop in and out   dying fishes   wide
expanse   aural oceanic   din but listening   dismissed as
noise   disguising plot

to lean together and do nothing
not kick a stone or even point out
the extraordinary or ordinary sky
to practice form
new witches they   long limbed and lissome   dodging and
crossing alone   in small groups and big   fox gloves drooping
bird sleeps   bird in the palm's hollows   to hold as well as
crush   shoulders serene in sockets   fluff   down   rotating
easily   setting off that caustic smell   bilingual   acrid
that decade
disturbing the hoardings storefront promised glossed
crisp bleach arches the nostrils
hock   sing   phlegm   ride
algae happens only blooming over stiller waters
bad organs of headless mice discarded
piss filled kidneys at the door
the chewed thing continues to get being chewed   provides
no nourishment   sucks out what little life   grows larger
unmanageable lump between jaws   mouth struggles   lump
near sentient   jaw aches   strains   beyond for the bones to
crack   dislocate   lump emerges as efficiency   takes from the
chewer its head
replaces it with itself
abandons for husk
what vessel

more capable deadly livelier
across the face of a woman
the face of a woman
over grimace film of another
not quite aligning
two faces   there are two   one on top one below   identical
expression   passing over   slight delay   blur   smear
burn   scar   appearance of transparency   lain over face
causing an extra quality of expression   itself with another
unrecognizable   impossible to identify   what is named
horror   (having to name)   peering from the platform at
Peckham Rye   perhaps it was just   still being alive
some new breathing curve swerving
braids flaring out carving space up
lit in this silver light moon outside Waterloo
street traffic glitz crane gleaming theater can rubble tent   piss
glass gutter bark pulse jump
this silver light
leaping preventing a landing
braids fly wing headless
this silver light
leaving luminous trails   outside the big station   yank mama's
hand   willing a wildness leaping   from beneath the feet
come on hot belly of earth   come on   before the train comes
crack   before the train comes   no chasm not to disappear

go in but ludicrous   high staked with long thighs   yank
mama's hand   come on crack   leap   break smash with the
feet come on no shadow's shadow   flesh   beast   intentions
the studied deference of workers and some children
the angles described by their bent knees curved backs
as they lean on walls to smoke during breaks
who wear their waste and the world's betrayal searingly as
an angle
of light
touches the face of your sleeping lover
unarguably as the skipped breath upon this sighting in the
morning or whenever that makes you
leap alive and yearn to die in
the same moment which like all others ends
so you rise
leap alive
in sharp and brilliant focus
open please   what violence is intimacy   still to come
this world   thin hunger   to clamp open   to climb inside
to brush against   to smell   love hound fool   to be fed
to plan and cook a meal together   to live alone or in groups
casual unstarved moisturized   in the street you were loved in
Coldharbour Lane 2004

you shall not afflict any widow or orphan if you afflict him at all
and if he does cry out to me I will surely hear his cry and my anger

will be kindled and I will kill you with the sword and your wives
shall become widows and your children fatherless
to open the back of a skull hinged upon long bone of nose
red gray   convolutions of brain   hand reaches to touch
bald red isosceles cuts
a pleat into the head   what need   when love is simply a good
smell   surrender the organs   lay them at shrines   tins of rings
of pineapple   bright plastic flowers   good carbonated drinks
oh proximity!

press
with fingers
a willing cheek
to find them plunged into wet orange sludge of city   goiters
of oak trees those mushrooms that strike out in ledges
insistent   horse   meat   pollen
a hand reaching out is a length
is travelling
is dormant intelligence   mouseish and chased
is arriving daily angrier poorer needier
after crossing the city for work or love's work
all desire now only for war   or to break the head open   on
the pavement with a hammer   with metal
with the hand a fist in the hair
an arid point of loss knows only its own belly   echoing
worked bony

drooling on the bus budgeting   hunger is only one feeling
with only one
dimension
oh   oh   longing
unapologetically
for any stranger   any park
for the air's precise smell to be: aniseed   fox shit   fried cheese
for the molten pink sky
for the exact temperature that was the truest bliss
for hash dripping from trees
for only the point of touch   this   *this*
over any drinking weekend   over any weekday sneak out
over rapid solvents   over tedium disguised as commitment
over terror disguised as maturity over shame disguised
as intellect   over   naming disguised as action
over grief disguised as the rage you cannot
name for it is the love you never knew
voter passenger worker beaten rabid frothed and bawling
solid globs of sweat pooling in the pits and troughs clump
horde obsessive compulsive circular circling vulture taking
aim   what big city   mangled cycles   crawling in queues for
tin and dirt   backs hunched tumorous mounds   humans
sleep in waste outside and perish   pressed into mouthlessness
hard for laying face down on a sofa thoroughly sciatic   no
one has ever known temperateness   its bliss   getting shoved

through the spasming bowel of forced participation squeezing
the mind's widths into the narrowest channel pressing the
intellect's imaginative capacity into a dream of the most enviable
holiday into jealousy and well-laid towns quelling the heart's
commodiousness into a pair of bouncing breasts attached or
not to any irrelevant being   where would animosity towards
monuments   triumphs against architecture fit   where are
the ruins of the castle   where is the cold sea   no space even
to assemble vengeance   capacities lapsed and loose as a fitful
colon   may this peak from below resemble a drop

androgynous bed time

probe the anus gently with a finger   meet in alleys   read
underline in orange pencil   when it is possible go online
arrange people together and then leave   make love the
distance between us   line the inside rims of eyelids   fall from
bridges

live anyway

headless

be the brick

the lovely mule

be wise

you can hurt too

pain is only a mouse under a rug   distorting the shape
trying only to get out b-roads   chalk pits   refineries   forests
oil   timber   new towns   gorse luminous against the blue

the underpass rent alleyway graffiti the streets in the
sky cancer dementia open air prisons the commuter
belt fey boys polyester haunches fingertips industrial
zones crowbars chemical warfare ordinary warfare police
shootings oranges evacuation the backseats of shit cars
grazes tramways skips drained lakes a sibling's bedroom
getting beaten up in small towns rubble the environmental
impact of glitter millions of spider webs in the grass fun
fur rape true love shift work uniforms hair-
nets the long number across the front the toxic
sea eviscerated schools illiteracy overcrowding skin
freckles overdrafts waiting lists housing circles
paws songs written nowhere mobile costing nothing
making a new language for a new world or a new world
from a new language articulates us backwards
echoes forwards resonates—

Yellow sludge is air. In chlorinated puffs smudging along the surface easily. Bullying line. Sleep easy now—but for the extra slop mussing the outlines, the nerves forced out in a blossom. Part sentient, holding a loose shape, familiar, grotesque. Crouching, crawling, old or young, dogs, an animal, stars, stoking organs in some undergrowth, probably mammalian, bloated or beached, reptilian, cloud, full of errors, ghosts, echoes. Dense thicket of big leaves heavy with green rain, lush and noxious. Fog, steeple, skyscraper, hill. Spring gutter, overflowing connector, gyratory thick with beings and forms. Smoke plume hangs in deep fried air. Paws, mammal probably or claws, feet, limbs out, these streets, a living room, den, mouth open, teeth bared, formless almost, full of dirt. Soft pads burn, tips and sensors. Refusing creatures in skinned contortions. Every no a yes to not-this. Listen—petals are unfurling, the blossoms lift and drop. Listen—the red face punches through, fist in a wall, chair upturned. Wind lifts a pelt. Cat food, beer, tampons, cream cheese, condoms. Shadeless horizon recurring. Cocks, weeds, genius mites. Sort of staccato—heat, gravity, heat. Mercurial motion, cinnabar bright. Squatting under a fat mushroom inhaling cement. Rattles inside. Eyes probably, mouths, limbs. Anxious track goes around and around arterial—but in a spiral, not a circle. Out. A vulture practices precision, not circling but soaring, pissing on its legs to kill carcass bacteria. Mush goes any way or none. But the ears. Something is being wrapped around the torsos. Drop into the wet city's orange ruins, heaving and sculpted. Curl under bowing the cartilage. Hinges open, close. Heads loll on the stack, pulling heavily on the attaching pieces. Tentacles, discs loosing, piles of feathers, calciums knocking. Hinges experience pressure. Muck full of medical waste, wrong water, amoebic palpitation. Lapping at twisting psychedelia slicking oily puddles. Metal boughs writhing parched into the sky-covering making sudden lacerations. Front limbs getting grazed, mud shards and mica. Fine matter splaying and thin. Dirt dirt and street dirt entering. Hinges burn, go towards their limits, quake. Mass has mass too. Little terror, no matter. Young abyss, no drinking water, no swifts. Wanting more than no time to tend, each busy gesture describing a hollow. Wanting more than what passes for love, that blood drawing clawed clutching at the surface terror. Constance strengthens the muscles, care makes sensible flesh—knowing love's work through loving all. Hot soil tar pavement squirms wetly collapsing in slow wideness and starting to rip and tear. A substance files in through the gaps and cuts, pouring confidently in, inflating all the areas and altering their shapes into what stands up, stands down. Wanted some air, to decide shape in. Something is being wound around the wrists and there is a hook in the flesh of the back attached to a rooted thing. But the ears. Can't get around, can't eat. Held in a held position. Slips over. Can't get around, can't eat. Ligaments or tissues or tendons shred and rent. To pull pulls the hook, tents the fresh skin, rips. Ear brain fills with this wrenching, blinds eyes. Mud in the gums. To know the scent of the gasping yellow rose. Six-hour journey, numerous delays, snow, arms, a blanket. Little tender raises to sick lips some liquid. Patch below reckons with being pressed. Clouds dust up all around, revealing. Surfaces raw with blood matted fur skin fluff hair feathers scale sores scabs bruises. Head bit dips up and down in a wave, opens its mouth beak face hole and splutters—half-syllables exit, it won't do, stutter, unrecognizable, peripheral, other, spit, it won't do, nervous encounter, soundless, vomit. Tongue tumorous and pressed up, pushed out, beyond its curve stretched from the back of the hole. Series of holes—pupils, nostrils, mouth, ears, bellybutton, pussy, arse, urethra. Something is being wrapped around the legs. But the ears. Sour lament for air. Others, smells, openings and closings, huddled close, toenails claws fill audibly with earth, scrabbling. Trees burst through fences and grow around them, iron buckles and bends. Being born and dying out of love. Food, shelter, water. Leaf's edges curving into air, pores open to dim light, thick gas. Roots chafing at earth, bug-full. Handsome larynx. Little worm adores invisible gases, breathes through its fine skin. Miraculous spiracle and tracheal tube taking the air deep into the beetle. Spider's elegant lamellae layered in fine pages and open to the world through abdominal slits. Pacific universe. Metal ring throbs around mechanic skull. Brittle defense. Distance from affection, from everything, enough. Fondling a rock all the light and dark hours, go on sing ha ha. Dig heels, dig tunnels under the world and out of it, smuggle perfume and medicine, escape. Inhalation of white phosphorous strips the insides out. Where the sky begins, an echo of skin, touch, untouch, little point of meeting. Pull this way push that, push this way pull that. Ordinary primary forces selection coupon. Nimble blockheads on all fours, doltish, probably

mammalian, winged. Paw put out, patch gives a little, bounces,
is pressed, gives, alters, is diggable, chafes. Thick material fraying
intensely there, here, at the pull of hook. A small gap forms regardless,
wet tarmac street tube. Traces over words. Sliver potent populated.
Mouth open to its widest point, emerges into crisp and aching
lilac web embracing. Stimulating the tendons which buttress out
disrupting the circumference into a breaking with no effort beyond
refusal, each creature tripping with the sweet thrill of living without
for a moment having wanted death. Radiating and retreating to the
pulse of involuntary effort—against itself, for itself, with nothing but
itself. There is a storm. Unplanned buckling realized only through
clunky dedication to all that is not wrapped around that which is
trying to move, to all that is not the lurid force felt fully, to all that
knows refusal is a kind of devotion. A dot among dots, infinite. Not
as but for. Edgeless. Moss. From the tiny scent, young apple, tar, soot,
tooth, paper, kiss, sleep, blood, saliva, small animal stretching, bullet,
chorus, to each pulsing universe glimpsed at the feeling limit of skin,
of all that is shared which is all there is. Every thing's and no thing's.
Audaciously. In love. Always and only. To lean is to stand against.
A stone, a stone is pulled from the mouth. Knowing and mottled,
studied, dirt brushed off, held. Lump of remembrance, brutal compass,
a mirror reflecting an impossible sky—tangible, all at once. A stone, a
stone is pulled from the mouth, pulled from the mouth and thrown.
Jaws open, hands open—breathing, breathing, here.

Notes

Some of the works the author read or thought with during the years of writing *Yes, I Am A Destroyer* are cited here. Sometimes the author has quoted directly from them or had been thinking of a particular line or passage when writing. In other instances, the texts have been written alongside, and not quoted from. The texts are listed alphabetically.

Theodor W. Adorno, "Memento," *Minima Moralia: Reflections From Damaged Life*, translated by E. F. N. Jephcott, London: Verso, 2005 (1951).

Nanni Balestrini, "Letter to My Unsuspecting, Peaceable Reader," translated by Neinsager, in *Anguish Language: Writing and Crisis*, edited by John Cunningham, Anthony Iles, Mira Mattar, Marina Vishmidt, Berlin: Archive Books, 2015 (2001).

Walter Benjamin, "On the Concept of History," 1940.

Jane Bowles, "Curls and a Quiet Country Face," *Jane Bowles: Collected Writings*, edited by Millicent Dillon, New York City, NY: Library of America, 2017 (fragment, early 1950s).

Anne Boyer, "Are We Often Seeing What is 'Untrue' as 'True': Anne Boyer on Poets and Lying," The Poetry Foundation, 13 August, 2012.

—."Formulary for a New Feeling," *A Handbook of Disappointed Fate*, Brooklyn, NY: Ugly Duckling Presse, 2018.

Bertolt Brecht, *The Tutor*, 1950, digitized by RevSocialist for Socialist Stories.

Brigid Brophy, *The King of a Rainy Country*, London: The Coelacanth Press, 2012 (1956).

Roger Caillois, "Mimicry and Legendary Psychasthenia," translated by John Shepley, *Minotaure* 7, Paris, 1935.

Julia Calver, *These Coins, My Eyes*, 2010. This pamphlet is held at the Women's Art Library, Goldsmiths University, London.

Anne Carson, "The Glass Essay," *Glass, Irony, and God*, London: Jonathan Cape, 1998.

Aimé Césaire, "Discourse on Colonialism," translated by Joan Pinkham, *Monthly Review Press*, New York & London, 1972 (1955).

Anton Chekov in a letter to A. S. Suvorin, 7 January, 1889, translated by Constance Garnett, *The Project Gutenberg EBook of Letters of Anton Chekhov*, 2004.

Clémence X. Clementine and Associates from the Infinite Venom Girl Gang, "Against the Couple Form," *LIES: A Journal of Materialist Feminism*, Volume 1, USA, 2012.

CA Conrad, *A Beautiful Marsupial Afternoon*, Seattle, WA: Wave Books, 2012.

Merce Cunningham, "Space, Time, and Dance," 1952.

Roque Dalton, "Toward a Better Love," translated by Jack Hirschman, *Clandestine Poems*, Evanston, IL: Curbstone Press, 1995 (1980).

Mahmoud Darwish, "Who am I without exile?," translated by Fady Joudah, *The Butterfly's Burden*, Port Townsend, WA: Copper

Canyon Press, 2007.
Angela Davis, *Freedom Is A Constant Struggle: Ferguson, Palestine, and the Foundations of a Movement*, Chicago, IL: Haymarket Books, 2016.
Amy De'Ath, "'Go in boys. Go in and stay there.' Feminist Poetry and Reading Dialectically," in *Anguish Language: Writing and Crisis*, edited by John Cunningham, Anthony Iles, Mira Mattar, Marina Vishmidt, Berlin: Archive Books, 2015.
Frére Dupont, *Species Being and Other Stories*, San Francisco, CA: Ardent Press, 2007.
Monsieur Dupont, *Nihilist Communism: A Critique of Optimism—the Religious Dogma that states there will be an Ultimate Triumph of Good over Evil—in the Far Left*, San Francisco, CA: Ardent Press, 2009 (2003).
Noura Erakat, "Whiteness as Property in Israel: Revival, Rehabilitation, and Removal," *Harvard Journal on Racial & Ethnic Justice*, Cambridge: MA, 2015
"Roundtable on Anti-Blackness and Black-Palestinian Solidarity," moderated by Noura Erakat, *Jadaliyya*, 3 June, 2015.
Frantz Fanon, *The Wretched of the Earth*, translated by Constance Farrington, London: Penguin Books, 2001 (1962).
Ida Faré and Franca Spirito, *Mara and the Others, quoted in Tiqqun, Sonogram of a Potentiality*, translated by Tiqqunista, Brooklyn, NY: Pétroleuse Press, 2011.
Claire Fontaine, *Human Strike Has Already Begun & Other Writings*,

London: Mute Books & the Post-Media Lab at Leuphana University, 2013.

Jean Genet, *Prisoner of Love*, translated by Barbara Bray, London: Picador, 1990 (1986).

Ursula K. Le Guin, *The Dispossessed*, 1974, London: Gollancz, 2002.

Stuart Hall, "Minimal Selves," in *The Real Me: Postmodernism and the Question of Identity*, ICA Documents 6, London: The Institute of Contemporary Arts, 1987.

Stefano Harney & Fred Moten, *The Undercommons: Fugitive Planning & Black Study*, Wivenhoe: Minor Compositions, 2013.

bell hooks, "Eating the Other: Desire and Resistance," *Black Looks: Race and Representation*, Boston, MA: South End Press, 1992.

Elfriede Jelinek, *Lust*, translated by Michael Hulse, London: Serpent's Tail, 1992 (1989).

Franz Kafka, source lost.

Margarita Karapanou, *Kassandra and the Wolf*, translated by N. C. Germanacos, New York & London: Harcourt Brace Jovanovich, 1974.

Robin D. G. Kelley, "An Anti-Racist Movement," *Social Text Online*, 13 November, 2016.

R. D. Laing, *The Divided Self*, London: Pelican, 1965 (1959).

Clarice Lispector, *Near to the Wild Heart*, translated by Alison Entrekin, Cambridge, MA: New Directions, 2012 (1943).

Carla Lonzi, "Let's Spit on Hegel," translated by Veronica Newman, New York: Secunda, 2010 (1970).

"Finding Resonances with Carla Lonzi," Giovanni Zapperi with Federica Bueti, *Makhzin*, Beirut, 1 April, 2016.

Andreas Malm, "The Walls of the Tank: On Palestinian Resistance," *Salvage*, 1 May, 2017.

Karl Marx, *Capital: Critique of Political Economy, Volume 1*, translated by Ben Fowkes, London: Penguin Books, 1990 (1867)

Joseph Massad, "The Cultural Work of Recovering Palestine," *boundary 2*, volume 42, issue 4, 2015.

Joni Mitchell, "Down to You," from the album *Court and Spark*, 1974.

Fred Moten, "blackpalestinian breath," *Social Text Online*, 25 October, 2018.

Annie Olaloku-Teriba, "Afro-Pessimism and the (Un)Logic of Anti-Blackness," *Historical Materialism*, issue 26 (2).

Sandeep Parmar, Nisha Ramayya and Bhanu Kapil, *Threads*, London: Clinic Publishing, 2018.

Fernando Pessoa/Álvaro de Campos, "Tabacaria," *Presença - Folha de Arte e Crítica*, Coimbra, 1933 (1928).

"Strategy for the Liberation of Palestine," published by the Popular Front for the Liberation of Palestine in February 1969. It was translated at that time by the PFLP Information Department.

Lisa Robertson, "On Form (for Jane Ellison)," *3 Summers*, Toronto: Coach House Books, 2016.

Edward Said, "Intellectual Exile: Expatriates and Marginals," in *Representations of the Intellectual: The 1993 Reith Lectures*, New York: Vintage, 1996.

The Edward Said Mixtape (Vol. 6): interview with Michaël Zeeman, *The East is a Podcast*, 17 September 2019.

Ella Shohat, "The Alphabet of Dispossession" and "Postscript to Frantz Fanon's *The Wretched of the Earth*," in *On the Arab-Jew, Palestine, and Other Displacements: Selected Writings*, London: Pluto Press, 2017.

Viktor Shklovsky, "Resurrection of the Word," in *Russian Formalism: A Collection of Articles and Texts in Translation*, translated by Richard Sherwood, edited by Stephen Bann and John E. Bowlt, New York: Barnes and Noble, 1973 (1914).

Tiqqun, *Sonogram of a Potentiality*, translated by Tiqqunista, Brooklyn, NY: Pétroleuse Press, 2011.

Trinh T. Minh-ha, *Woman, Native, Other:Writing Postcoloniality and Feminism*, Bloomington, IN: Indiana University Press, 1989.

Bechaela Walker, *The blank, stupid face of a tourist*, London: Monster Emporium Press, 2017.

Simone Weil—sources lost.

Frank B. Wilderson III, "Afro-pessimism & the End of Redemption," *Occupied Times*, 30 March, 2016.

"'We're trying to destroy the world' Anti-Blackness & Police Violence After Ferguson. An Interview with Frank B. Wilderson III," Ill Will Editions, November 2014.

Monique Wittig, "One is Not Born a Woman," *The Straight Mind and Other Essays*, Boston, MA: Beacon Press, 1992.

The Book of Exodus 22:23, The Bible, King James version.

Extracts

Portions of this work have appeared in the following publications:

"Digital Poetics #29 *Yes, I Am A Destroyer* (Extract) by Mira Mattar w/ Essay from Kashif Sharma-Patel." *the87press: theHythe*, August 24, 2021.

"*Yes, I Am A Destroyer* (Excerpt) — Mira Mattar." *minor literature[s]*, January 26, 2021.

[Untitled Extract.] In *Doyenne 02: Singing To Spirits*, edited by Flora Yin Wong. Doyenne, 2023. https://doyenne-books.bandcamp.com/merch/d-02-singing-to-spirits

[Untitled Extract.] Translated by Elsa Boyer. *Senna Hoy* 11 (July 2022). Edited by Luc Bénazet and Jackqueline Frost.

[Untitled Extract.] Translated by Elene Abashidze. *Danarti* 20 (April 2024). Edited by Anuka Ramischwili-Schafer and Kashif Sharma-Patel.

Acknowledgments

My gratitude to Julia Calver, John Cunningham, Karim Mattar, Hestia Peppé, Michael Reid, and Bechaela Walker for reading and commenting on the manuscript at various stages, and for their encouragement and friendship; to Julia Hodgson and Kate Hughes for kindly allowing the reproduction of their art works; to Susan Finlay and Susan Fletcher for their advice on publishing; and to Sharon Kivland for her kindness and patience, for her rigorous engagement with my writing, and for her editorial wisdom.

For their friendship, support, and inspiration I thank Phoebe Blatton, Josephine Berry, Darsavini, Lidija Haas, Jennifer Hodgson, Emilia McKenzie, Ainhoa Montoya, Judy Moore, Pauline van Mourik Broekman, and Catherine Scott—dearly departed; to my south London family for the love we continue to share; to the *Mute / Metamute* collective; to Liz Murray and Sam Basu of Treignac Projet for giving me space to write; to my parents for more than I can put into words; and of course to dear Olive, who, being feline, thankfully will never have to read this book.

Finally, I saw the words "Yes I Am A Destroyer" painted faintly on a wall at which I was staring at the Performing Arts Forum in France during the summer of 2019 while trying to write something entirely different. Thank you to the painter of those words.